THE
LOST
MINE

To Ray
Best Wishes

[signature]

THE

LOST MINE

PAUL RIMMASCH

DIGITAL LEGEND

Published by:
Digital Legend Press and Publishing
A subsidiary of Legends Library Publishing, Inc.
Rochester, NY / Cottonwood Heights, UT
www.DigitaLegend.com
info@digitalegend.com
877-222-1960

ISBN: 978-1-937735-59-3

Printed in the United States of America

Cover art by Mac McCann

Cover and interior designed by Jacob Frandsen

To my Scoutmaster, Larry

FACT:

In the summer of 1852, Thomas Rhoades, a veteran of the War of 1812, left Salt Lake City on an errand of great importance for The Church of Jesus Christ of Latter Day Saints. Two weeks later, he returned from the rugged Uintah Mountains with approximately sixty-two pounds of pure gold. This was his first of many such trips. The precious metal was a gift to the cash-strapped church from the Ute Chief Wakara. The gold came from a mine sacred to the Ute people, which they called Carre-Shinob. Thomas Rhoads swore an oath promising never to reveal the location of the mine. To this day, the whereabouts of Carre-Shinob remains one of Utah's greatest mysteries.

But before ye seek for riches, seek ye for the kingdom of God.

Jacob 2:18
The Book of Mormon

1

Tlahuicle paused, then turned and looked back down the long cause-way. He wanted to gaze at the imperial city of Tenochtitlan one last time. He had always loved the way its walls reflected in the waters of the lake. Its appearance was as magical as the story of its founding. A tear welled up in his eye. He knew that he would not see it again.

"What does it matter?" he said aloud. His beloved Acaxochitl was dead, cut down by the filthy pale men from across the sea. Furthermore, his civilization was about to die. The demon Cortez was gone, but he would return. He would return to destroy all that was sacred to the Aztec people.

"I will not let that happen," he promised, fingering a gold necklace trimmed with quetzal feathers, a last gift from his wife.

His master, Montezuma, had honored him, the most faithful of all of his servants, with a special task: thwart the grasping plans of Cortez, a task from which he and those who traveled with him would never return.

Tlahuicle heaved a sigh, and turned his face once again to the north. With a heavy heart, he resumed his journey toward the land of his ancestors.

2

Present Day

The two children squealed with delight as their parents pushed them higher and higher on the old metal park swings. The boy, who looked approximately eight years of age, pumped his legs, trying to get the most out of his mother's effort. The girl, two or so years his junior, was content to go with the flow. The parents were enjoying this respite from the hectic pace of their lives. Smiling contentedly, they tried to discuss their hopes and plans for the future over the happy noise of their children.

Of this blissful family scene, Donald Kress saw only the mother. As he stood hidden in the trees at the edge of the city park, Donald marveled at her beauty. She was even more beautiful than in his memories. Motherhood suited her well. She was full of a grace and poise she had not processed thirteen years ago. He felt a lump rise in his throat. Not wanting to show weakness to the two dark-skinned men standing silently a few paces behind him, he turned and in a harsh voice said, "I've seen enough, gentlemen. It's time to go."

"Where we goin', Boss?" the shorter and stockier of the two questioned.

"Simple, Arapeen," Donald replied with a cruel smile. "To find John Byrd."

3

Ammon Rogers had faced death in battle in Iraq, had almost fallen into a pit of angry rattlesnakes, and had once come within inches of being shot off the side of a cliff by an unknown enemy. None of these experiences filled him with as much dread as the task now before him: his third Elders Quorum "move" of the week.

When he had looked President Fitzhume in the eyes and agreed to accept the calling of Elders Quorum President, he had thought he was accepting a spiritual calling. He thought he was going to be teaching lessons, going to meetings, and giving counsel. He had no idea that he was being called to be CEO of *Rogers Moving and Storage*. Now he understood why his wife and friends had offered him condolences instead of congratulations.

I guess that was another thing growing up more active in the LDS church would have given me a clue about, he thought, sighing in resignation.

It was not only the piles of elderly Sister Henderson's unpacked belongings that made him feel gloomy; it was the pressures of what his mother called "grown-up life." There were simply a lot of things that worried a married man that a single student, or even a single soldier, did not think about twice. Marriage was not the problem: the past year with Sariah had been amazing. Every morning when he opened his eyes and saw her, it was like seeing her for the first time.

Except, he reminded himself with a laugh, *she's not standing at the front door of my dorm shouting in my face. Besides that, it's like seeing her for the first time.*

Nevertheless, he did feel guilty at times. Sariah had thrown herself into marriage and had tried to become the picture of domestic perfection. Ammon could tell, however, that she missed parts of her old adventurous life, combing the world for archaeological proof of the Book of Mormon with her father. As Ammon loaded yet another box of empty Cool Whip containers onto the U-Haul truck, the blue and red tubs reminded him of the first time his parents came over for dinner. Sariah wanted to make everything perfect and had spent all morning trying to make a molten chocolate soufflé. When Ammon came home from school, the house was full of smoke and Sariah was half laughing and half crying. The Cool Whip she had purchased to top the desert was the only part of the enterprise unburnt.

"I do much better with Dutch ovens!" she said, dipping her finger in the whipped topping and eating it, her face streaked with flour.

Ammon kissed her on the forehead, indulged himself with his own finger of Cool Whip, and replied, "Why don't you make Dutch oven, then?"

His parents had thoroughly enjoyed the ribs and cobbler, but the incident was a prime illustration of her struggles. The far-off look that came into her eyes every time the women of the ward engaged her in conversations about the latest sale at Old Navy, soccer practice, or other domestic concerns, told Ammon that Sariah was not there. She was thinking about scaling pyramids in South America or scuba diving to sunken ruins off the coast of Bimini. That look made him feel like he had taken a wild and free songbird and put her into a cage.

"It's a shabby cage at that," he said aloud, loading another box into the truck. He paused a moment and rubbed his aching lower back.

Money was another one of his worries. As a single student, he had gotten along quite well on his G.I. bill and a little help from his parents. Now that he was married, all of that was different. They had both needed to take jobs, and Sariah had quit school. Ammon's beloved Book of Mormon teacher, Professor Millbarge, had found Sariah a job at the BYU Library, and Ammon had taken a part time position at a local athletic training facility working with young football players. This all helped them to make ends meet, but it did not even scratch the surface of what he really wanted to do.

Ammon still had in his possession the fragments of glowing stone he and Sariah had removed from a cave high in the Grand Canyon. He so desperately wanted to conduct research and figure out what made them glow. Such a study could yield new sources of energy and change the world. Almost every night, he removed the largest fragment from its protective case under his bed and gazed into its light. He marveled at how, even after thousands of years and sustaining severe damage, it still shone bright and clear. If only he could unlock its secrets. The trouble was, he could not just march into his physics class and analyze it. Doing so would raise too many questions—questions he had been instructed not to raise.

What Ammon really needed for the project was money. With a few pieces of key equipment, he could make a study of his own. Unfortunately, they did not sell used mass spectrometers at Deseret Industries. Ammon had suggested that Sariah ask her father, John Byrd, for help buying, but she had insisted that they make their own way in life. The only thing she would accept from her father was the house in the older part of Provo, which he had given them as a wedding present. *Ah, yes. The house*, he thought.

The first room Sariah had picked out was the nursery. After over a year of marriage, however, the nursery was still empty. Sariah did not let on that it bothered her, but Ammon had found her softly crying more than once.

Ammon paused and surveyed the scene; just a few more things to load into the truck, although, in his opinion, they should throw away the remaining junk, not move it. He took a drink from the garden hose and got back to work. Ammon hoped he would be done in time for dinner.

Going back inside Sister Henderson's house, Ammon saw an old cloth-covered wooden case with a handle on top. Without paying attention, he grabbed the handle and lifted. The case was heavier than he expected. As he moved toward the front door, the bottom of the case suddenly crashed to the floor. Embarrassed, Ammon looked timidly to the floor. An antique sewing machine lay awkwardly on the carpet. Ammon looked at the lid still in his hands, and mentally kicked himself.

I should have checked the latches! he thought.

Something caught his eye. Stuffed inside the top of the lid were some papers. Ammon reached into the lid and removed them. The two folded papers looked old. He unfolded the documents. Hand-written numbers, lines, and words covered the paper on top. It resembled a makeshift cross-word puzzle. The bottom paper was a crudely drawn map. Written at various locations on the map were strange symbols. Ammon made out trees, mountain peaks, rivers, and a lake, but he ignored the topographical features. What caught his attention, however, was a hand drawn X to the upper left of the lake, with two words written above it that Ammon had never seen before: *Carre-Shinob*.

4

From his resting place under the large tree, Tlahuicle had a clear view of the changing landscape. Gone was the harsh and open desert. In its place was a land Tlahuicle could not have imagined in his wildest dreams, a land of narrow canyons, red rocks spires and arches. He and his companions had traveled far, but they still had many days journey ahead.

If we stay on this ancient trail and follow its markers, we will reach our destination, he thought. *Then I will have completed my mission. Then I can rest.*

He removed the necklace his beloved had given him and gazed at the worn and faded quetzal feathers. The long dusty road had taken as much of a toll on the feathers as it had on him. Tlahuicle wiped the dust from the golden image of the god Quetzalcoatl. Nothing could dim its shine, just as nothing dimmed his memories of the lovely Acaxochitl. A sad smile crept across his face. She had looked radiant the day she had given him the necklace. Adorned in quetzal feathers, gold, and jewelry in preparation to dance in the great festival, she had placed the necklace around his neck, kissed him gently, and told him that this gift was to remind him of the gift she wanted most of all: the gift of a child. She would never receive a gift now. During the great dance, without warning, the Spanish had become enraged and had—had—

Tlahuicle could not bear to remember. He stood, stretched his back, and called his men to order. They needed to get farther north before the winter came. The seven sacred caves were awaiting them.

Donald Kress looked in the rearview mirror as the large hospital slipped out of view. He barked out a harsh laugh. He could not believe how easy it had been to achieve his goal.

It would have been harder to steal a spare blanket from the supply closet he thought. All he had done was dress like a janitor, slipped into the hospital late at night, and acted as if he knew what he was doing.

Donald focused his attention back on the road ahead and hove a contented sigh. His plans for John Byrd had already been set in motion. Now, using the contents of the metal case tucked safely in the trunk of this car, he would not only exact revenge on the people who had held him captive for thirteen years, but on the church they served, as well.

6

Travis Stanwick forced a thin smile as he handed the customer the five dollars and twenty-eight cents change he was due. He insincerely wished him a good day and watched him exit the store.

Gotta be nice, he thought bitterly. *I need this job. I need something to go right in my life. The Rock Shop* on State Street in Salt Lake City was the only kind of place in which years of treasure hunting in the Uintah Mountains left him equipped to work. He had no money, no friends, no family—no one he even remotely trusted—but he did know rocks and minerals. Unfortunately for Travis, the less valuable a rock or mineral was, the better he knew it.

Travis reflected gloomily on his wasted life. As a boy, his grandfather had filled his head with campfire stories of the fabulous wealth hidden in the mountains to the east. The gold had seemed so close—just within his reach. Stories of Indians, conquistadors, friars, pioneers, and lost mines had fired his imagination so much that he left school in his teens and became a full-time treasure hunter. Spurred on by the old tales, he read numerous books on the subject and spent the rest of his time wandering the hills looking for gold. When his father died and left him a small inheritance, his mother begged him to settle down and get an education. He refused and blew the money on fruitless expeditions. Multiple unpaid loans alienated him from the rest of his family and friends. One wife, and then another, and another one after that, had all wanted a home and family from him. They each, in-turn, grew weary of hearing his oft-quoted promise, "Just one more trip: I know I will find the treasure this time."

He really could not blame them. Twenty years of searching gained him only misery. Still, he could not let his dreams go. The gold had to be out there somewhere. He even spent time among the Ute Indians who lived near the Uintahs, hoping to glean some information. They always denied knowing anything about lost gold, though he suspected they did.

Taking this job was, in a way, the last roll of the dice for him. Travis had run out of ideas and options, but maybe some rock hound trying to sell something would tip him off, or another treasure hunter coming in the store might slip up and spill the beans. The slightest hint could help lead him to the mother lode.

Travis knew this was extremely unlikely, but it was worth a try. Treasure hunters were a paranoid and suspicious bunch. They were not like photographers, motorcyclists, or other groups of people with similar interests, who formed clubs, had picnics, and shared information. In the best cases, there was simmering competition and mistrust. In the worst cases, there was open hostility and even bloodshed. Butch Cassidy and members of his gang even had their place in the lore of lost Utah mines.[1] Treasure hunters were, for the most part, desperate men and women just like him. They were always looking under "one more rock" in an attempt to salvage their broken dreams, always looking over their shoulders, afraid to lose what they did not have.

So far, Travis' hopes of finding out any new information had been in vain. He had not heard anything of interest at all. In fact, people had sought him out, trying to find out what he knew. He did not care enough to try to dissuade these newcomers from engaging on their own fool's errands. Like the Spanish before them, this generation would find its own ruin on the road to El Dorado.

Lost in his thoughts, Travis did not look up when the bell chimed, indicating the arrival of a new customer. He heard someone walk toward the front counter, but remained absorbed in counting the trilobites in the glass case below. When the man spoke, however, Travis snapped his head up so fast it hurt. It was not only what he said that got his attention; it was how he said it.

"Hey, you buy gold?" the young man asked in what Travis instantly recognized as a Ute accent.

"Where did the old woman say her father received the map?" John Byrd asked his son-in-law as he examined the paper closely.

"She said he found it stuffed inside the lid of a sewing machine he bought from a traveling salesman," Ammon responded, still smiling at the unexpected arrival of his father-in-law. Intrigued by his discovery, Ammon had asked Sister Henderson if he could borrow the documents, with the intention of showing them to John. To Ammon's great delight, she had insisted that he simply take them, going on about "those fool things" ruining her father's life and how, had she known she still possessed them, she would have tossed them into the fire.

As quickly as he could, Ammon finished the move, and rushed home to call John. John, fortuitously, was already there. It still amused Ammon how John disappeared for weeks, even months, and then suddenly showed up with some amazing new tale. Ammon thoroughly enjoyed these visits. Sariah craved them.

"That seems so random," Sariah interjected.

"It does, but it doesn't," John said, turning the map upside down and holding it up to the kitchen light. "I want to say that there is something about sewing machines in the lore of Carre-Shinob."

"What *is* Carre-Shinob?" Ammon asked.

"What is Carre-Shinob, indeed?" John responded, putting the paper down and looking Ammon straight in the eyes. "*Carre-Shinob* the word means 'Where the Great Spirit Dwells' to the Ute Indians. *Carre-Shinob* the place is one of the possible hiding places of Montezuma's lost treasure."

"Montezuma's lost treasure? I've heard of Montezuma's Revenge before, but never about a lost treasure," Ammon quipped.

When he saw his wife and father-in-law both open their mouths to speak, he quickly cut them off. "Are you both about to ask me, in your customary exasperated fashion, whether or not I ever attended Primary?" Ammon asked, with only partially feigned annoyance.

John and Sariah stood open-mouthed for a second, and then began to laugh.

"No, silly," Sariah said, still chuckling. "No *good* Primary teacher would mix Montezuma's lost treasure into their lesson."

"I would," John replied, wounded.

"Yes, father." Sariah hooked arms with John and added soothingly, "And that is why you are, as a general rule, kept away from small children."

As John and Sariah laughed again, Ammon came to his defense. "Hey, if I'd had a teacher like you growing up, I think I'd have gone to Primary more often."

"Thank you, son," John said triumphantly. "No respect from my own offspring."

"Nevertheless," he continued, "Sariah is correct. You probably never heard about the lost treasure in Primary. You probably never heard about it in history class either, which, in my opinion, you should have. But that is a different matter."

"Are you going to tell me, then?" Ammon asked.

"I would love to tell you—after we get some ice cream. I just got into town, you know," John replied, with a wink.

Sitting in the BYU Creamery again brought a flood of memories to Ammon Rogers. It was here, watching John Byrd eating Brigham's Beehive Crunch ice cream, as he was now, that Ammon's life had changed. All he had done was ask his Book of Mormon instructor, Professor Millbarge, a simple question, which became the catalyst for a meeting with John in this very ice cream shop. That meeting launched him on an adventure leading him to his two greatest treasures: his beloved wife and shards of one of the glowing stones lit by the finger of the Lord, the light that comforted the Jaredites in the darkness. Ammon smiled and took the scene before him in.

It was not until John had eaten about half of his bowl that he felt like continuing their discussion.

"All right. We were talking about our old friend Montezuma," John said contentedly.

"Yes. You were going to tell me about Montezuma's lost treasure," Ammon said, taking a bite of his own Marionberry ice cream. "Wasn't Montezuma a ruler in ancient Mexico?"

"Not just any ruler," Sariah responded. "He was the absolute ruler of the Aztecs in the first two decades of the fourteenth century."

"Good memory," John said. "There were many tribes in what is now called Mexico, but the Aztecs were the most powerful and the most feared."

"And the richest," Sariah added.

"Very true," John nodded. "Montezuma ruled his empire from the capitol city of Tenochtitlan, which was built on an island on Lake Texcoco. The city was one of the marvels of the world in that age. With a population of well over one hundred thousand, it rivaled any city in the world. It contained amazing architecture and fabulous wealth."

"Yeah, fabulous wealth which led Hernan Cortes to Tenochtitlan like a moth to a flame," Sariah said, polishing off the last of her ice cream.

"Cortes? He was a conquistador, right?" Ammon asked.

"Yes." John leaned back in his chair. "In 1519, the Spanish adventurer Hernan Cortes marched on Tenochtitlan with a small army, intent on ripping the wealth of the Aztecs from them. He did it in the name of God and the king and, of course, his own insatiable greed. It's ironic, really; Montezuma commanded a massive army and with one word could have wiped the Spaniards off the face of the earth."

"Why didn't he?" Ammon asked, intrigued.

"Simple," John said, with a wry smile. "Montezuma thought Cortes was a god."

"Oh, yeah. I remember something about that from school," Ammon tapped his spoon on the edge of his bowl. "What I don't remember is why."

"The Aztecs believed their ancestors had been visited by the god Quetzalcoatl, who arrived from the east and taught the people great wisdom. When he left, he promised to return one day," John said. "Their tradition said Quetzalcoatl had white skin and a beard. Cortes was the first such man they had ever seen—not to mention the fact that he arrived from the east," John said, with a smile.

"White skin, beard, came from the east, taught the people, promised to return…That sounds familiar," Ammon replied, smiling as well.

"Yes it does, doesn't it?" John chuckled. "The Quetzalcoatl story, with its parallels to Christ's visit to the Nephites, is usually the first 'evidence' that Book of Mormon scholars like to point at."

"That is especially true of the camp who points to Central America as the location of where the Book of Mormon takes place," Sariah added.

"True," John nodded.

"What happened to the Aztecs, then?" Ammon asked.

"Well," John continued, "Cortes and his men showed up at Tenochtitlan, and the Aztecs essentially gave him the key to the city. Cortes made himself at home, placed Montezuma under house arrest, and demanded the Aztecs bring all of their gold and silver to him."

"Did they do it?" Ammon asked.

"Some," John replied. "The majority of their treasure, however, was hidden in secret vaults beneath the palace.[2] At that point, Cortes' display of greed began to make some of the Aztecs doubt his divinity."

"Did the Spanish suspect the trick?" Ammon questioned.

"Yes, they did," John responded, "but Cortes soon had other things to worry about. The governor of Cuba sent an army to take Mexico for himself, and Cortes had to go and defend his conquests. He left only a few men behind, under the command of a trusted lieutenant."

"Pedro de Alvarado," Sariah interjected.

"Yes," John continued. "Alvarado was to hold the city and search for the treasure the Spaniard suspected was being kept from them."

"Did they find it?"

"They never got a chance," Sariah interjected. "While Cortes was away fighting the Spanish, the Aztecs held their annual festival honoring Huitzilopochtli, the Aztec god of war.

"As they had done for generations, hundreds of dancers arrayed splendidly in quetzal feathers and wearing gold and jewels took to the streets," John said. "The sight of all of the jewelry which had not been turned over to them threw the Spaniards into a rage."

"What did they do, take it from them?" Ammon asked.

"No! At least, not at first," Sariah said. "First they killed every last one of the dancers, and then they took the jewelry."

"Wow, that's harsh," Ammon said, uttering a low whistle.

"Well, the Conquistadors weren't exactly known for their subtlety," John added, leaning forward in his chair. "This brutal act effectively showed the Aztecs once and for all that the Spaniards were not, in fact, gods. They revolted. Alvarado and his men retreated inside a walled compound where they held the Aztecs at bay and waited for Cortes to return.

"Cortes had defeated the other Spanish army and was resting when he got word of the uprising. He quickly started back toward Tenochtitlan, where he eventually put down the revolt and became the unquestioned ruler of Mexico," John finished.

"But he never got the treasure?" Ammon asked.

"No," Sariah added. "Ol' Montezuma had one last trick up his sleeve."

"Before Cortes returned," John continued, "Montezuma ordered his servant—"

"Tlahuicle,"[3] Sariah interjected.

"Yes," John smiled briefly at her. "He ordered Tlahuicle and over a thousand porters to take the treasure out of the city, transport it far to the north to the ancestral homeland of the Aztecs, and hide it in seven sacred caves, where tradition said much of the gold came from in the first place."

"Did Cortes find out and go after the treasure?" Ammon asked.

"He heard rumors about it," John responded. "In fact, the seven sacred caves full of hidden treasure morphed into the Spanish legend of the seven gold-filled cities of Cibola, for which they unsuccessfully searched for the next two-plus centuries."

Ammon thought for a moment. "Wait a minute!" he exclaimed. "You said the ancestral homeland of the Aztecs was far to the north and not in Mexico."

"Correct," John replied. "Even mainstream historians acknowledge the Aztecs were not originally from Mexico."[4]

"Where did they come from, then?"

"There's good evidence they came from right here in Utah," Sariah responded.

"Utah! What kind of evidence?" Ammon asked skeptically.

"Well, there's linguistic evidence, for one," Sariah paused to remember. "The Aztecs spoke the dialect Nahuatl, which is closely related to the language spoken by the Ute Indians of northern Utah."

"Furthermore," John joined in, "the Aztecs themselves stated that their ancestors came from a land far to the north where they had lived on an island on a great inland sea. The word 'Aztec' comes from the word 'Aztlan,' meaning both "Island of Herons' and "White Land," which could describe the Great Salt Lake and the surrounding salt flats."[5]

"Their legends also say that to the east of their ancient island home was a range of mountains sacred to their ancestors," Sariah added. "That could easily be the Wasatch and Uintah Mountains."

"When did the Aztecs come to Mexico?" Ammon asked.

"They came sometime in the late tenth century or early eleventh century," John replied.

"Speaking of the Aztecs coming to Mexico," Sariah interjected, "here's some trivia for you: do you know where the image on the Mexican flag comes from?"

"No," Ammon said, slowly.

"You don't know what's on the Mexican flag, do you?" Sariah asked.

Ammon shook his head sheepishly.

"It's an eagle with a snake in its mouth, standing on a cactus," Sariah said.

"Oh, now that you mention it, I guess I have noticed that."

"Anyway, when the Aztecs came to Mexico, they were looking for a place to build a city. When they got to the shores of Lake Texcoco they saw, on one of the islands, an eagle perched on a cactus with a snake in its mouth. Their priests took this as a magical sign from their gods and they founded a city on that island that eventually became Tenochtitlan. The Mexican flag references that event."

"I was not aware of that," Ammon admitted.

Ammon thought a moment, his forehead creased. "Let me ask something. You said that some Book of Mormon scholars like to point at the Quetzalcoatl/Jesus connection as proof that the Book of Mormon lands were in or around Central America."

"Correct," John responded, finishing off his ice cream.

"Well," Ammon continued, "if the Aztecs didn't come to Mexico until a thousand years *after* Christ appeared to the Nephites, then isn't it logical to assume that they brought this belief with them, from the north?"

John blinked hard two times and said, "That's a good point. I have never thought of it like that before. I suppose they could have co-opted the belief in Quetzalcoatl from the local tribes they had conquered. Hmmm…that is a very good point, son. I think we will make a Forbidden Archaeologist out of you yet."

"Aww… Ammon," Sariah said placing her head on his shoulder.

"What?" He asked, amused.

"You're becoming one of us," she replied, affectionately

"Great!" Ammon said with pretend dread, and the three of them laughed.

"So let me get this straight," Ammon continued, after they ordered another round of ice cream. "You're saying that Montezuma's lost treasure was hidden somewhere here in Utah."

"Basically," John said.

"And the Spanish never found the treasure, even after two hundred years?"

"Nope," John said. "And it was more like *three* hundred years. They looked really hard, but the Indians kept the location secret from them, even though many paid for their defiance with their lives. They did not even like to talk about it with the white men. The caves were sacred to them. As the years went on, Montezuma's lost treasure melted from reality and into the realm of myth and legend."

"How do we even know the treasure still exists?"

"Oh, that is easy!" John said, with a broad smile and a wink. "The Indians told the Mormons about it."

9

1520 A.D.

Tlahuicle stood on the shores of the lake and watched the villagers fishing. The people were busily preparing for winter. Turning around, he looked up at the mountain that the Nuche people called Timpanocutiz. Snow already covered the tops of the peaks. With satisfaction, he noted that Timpanocutiz was an Aztec word, meaning 'the stone person.'[6] The mountain, indeed, looked like a woman lying on her back. This was proof to him that he was in the right place. He had reached the lands of his ancestors.

When Tlahuicle and his men arrived at the village by the lake, the Tumpanawach band of the Nuche people had welcomed them as long-lost cousins. Fortunately, their languages were still similar enough that they could communicate without great difficulty. Tlahuicle had wanted to continue his journey to the sacred caves immediately, but the Elders convinced him the mountain passes to the east would soon be snow-bound and impassable.

Eager as he was to complete his sacred mission, he saw the wisdom in their council. He and his men stayed the winter with the Tumpanawach and rested. They had traveled far and been burdened with much, but they were close to the end of the 'Trail of the Old Ones.' When the snow melted, they would go on and finish the task given to them by his master, Montezuma. Tlahuicle nodded with resignation, turned and, thinking of his beloved Acaxochitl, watched the children playing in the waters of the lake.

10

"They told the Mormons about the treasure?" Ammon asked skeptically.

"Yes," John replied.

"Really?" he persisted, skeptically.

"Yes."

"You make it sound like the Native Americans just rode into Salt Lake City one day, went right up to Brigham Young himself, and told him their secret!" Ammon laughed.

"Yes, that's more or less what happened. It was the 14th of June, 1849," John responded calmly.

Ammon looked with amazement from John to Sariah. She simply smiled and nodded.

"Oh, I gotta hear this story," Ammon said leaning forward on the table.

"And you shall," John said raising his right eyebrow slightly. "But first we have to back up a wee bit for contextual purposes."

"Of course."

"As I said, after the treasure disappeared into the north, the Spanish spent the next several hundred years looking for it, as well as for other mineral wealth. It was a dark time for the Indians."

"How so?" Ammon asked.

"Many were enslaved by the Spanish, only to die working in the mines. Others were forced to capture their brothers, to sell to the Spanish," John continued. "Disease, war, and bloodshed followed for many generations. Although thousands of pounds of gold and silver poured out of the Americas bound for Spain, Montezuma's treasure was never located. Of all the many tribes, the Utes were one of the most powerful, and they actually held the Spanish somewhat at bay. Oh, there was plenty of loss of life on both sides, but the Utes did pretty well for themselves."

"Wow, I didn't know that," Ammon responded.

"It's unfortunate, really," Sariah joined. "The Ute people have an amazing history and they only get, at best, a few lines in the history books."

"True," John said, nodding. "Back to the story: into this world, in about 1808, a Ute—I guess you would call him a prince—named Pan-a-Carre Quinker was born."

"Whoa, I thought my name was bad," Ammon said with a snort.

"Yes, Ute names are a mouth-full for us Anglos. It means 'Iron Twister.' Interestingly enough, Ute names surround the citizens of Utah, even though the vast majority of them do not know it. Many of the interesting place names here derive from Ute words. Why, in Pan-a-Carre Quinker's family alone, we have his grandfather San Pete and brothers Tabiona and Kanosh."

"Don't forget his other brother named Ammon!" Sariah reminded her father.

"Really? Ammon? Is that a Native American name?" Ammon asked.

"Not typically, but maybe you were both named after the same guy," John added, never missing an opportunity to make a point. "But I digress. Going on: into this world of strife our young prince was born. As he grew into adulthood, he, like most young people, began to question his place in the world. What destiny did the Great Spirit—?"

"Towats. That's what they called him," Sariah added.

"Yes. What destiny did Towats have for him? In order to find his answers, Pan-a-Carre Quinker traveled deep into the Uintah Mountains to a place sacred to his people, a lake named, appropriately, Spirit Lake. There he fasted, prayed, and chanted, hoping for direction from on high."

"What happened?" Ammon asked.

"At first, nothing," John continued. "Then, after several days, Towats appeared to him in a vision."

"Cool!" Ammon said. "What did he say?"

"Well, first, the Great Spirit changed his name," John replied.

"Proof that God is merciful," Ammon said with a chuckle.

"Stop!" Sariah elbowed Ammon in the ribs. "Show some respect."

"Sorry."

"Yes, well," John proceeded with his own chuckle. "Towats told him that from that time forward he would be known as Yah-keerah which means "The Keeper of the Yellow Metal."

"Yellow metal? Gold?" Ammon asked.

"Yes, gold," John said, nodding.

"Why did He give him that name?" Ammon asked.

"Towats gave him this name because it was at this time that He showed him the location of Carre-Shinob. Towats made him the protector of the gold it contained. Not only that, but He made Yah-keerah the guardian of the sacred relics belonging to his ancestors[7] that were hidden therein."

"The relics of his ancestors? You mean—?" Ammon said.

"Montezuma's lost treasure. Yes," Sariah finished his sentence.

Ammon made a low whistle.

"That's not even the coolest part," Sariah said.

"Really?" Ammon responded.

"Well," John joined. "The Great Spirit instructed him to keep the secret until he met a group of people Towats called the 'High Hats.' Yah-keerah was to share the treasure with them, and only them, because they would use the gold in a manner that would please Towats."

"High Hats? Who the heck were they?" Ammon asked, scratching his head.

"That was the trouble: Yah-keerah didn't know," John said. "Based on the long violent history the Utes and the Spanish shared, he knew they were not the ones, even though their friars sometimes wore tall pointy hats. He thought it might be the mountain men, but they only cared about furs and were not interested in gold."

"The mountain men did give Yah-keerah the name by which we know him today," Sariah added.

"The poor guy got another name change?" Ammon said.

"Not really," John said. "They—and I think you can sympathize—had trouble pronouncing Ute names. Yah-keerah came out more like Wakara.

That eventually morphed into Walker. He had become a chief by then. They called him Chief Walker, the name he is most often referred to to-day."

"Oh yeah, that is much easier to say," Ammon said, with relief. "Who were the High Hats, then?"

"For years, Walker had no idea," John continued. "Then one day, he had another vision. In this vision, Towats carried Walker high above the clouds and showed him trains of covered wagons crossing the plains. The men with the wagons were wearing top hats made of silk or fur."

"Mormon pioneers!" Ammon exclaimed.

"That is right, son. Towats told Yah-Keerah that these people were the 'High Hats' for which he waited. He pointed out one man in particular and told Walker to reveal the secret of Carre-Shinob to him. Walker asked when this man would come. Towats simply replied, 'Soon'."

"Who was the man? Brigham Young?" Ammon asked.

"No," John answered, enjoying Ammon's suspense.

"Who, then?"

"I am coming to that part," John responded. "On June 14th, 1849, Walker and a band of Utes rode into Salt Lake City and requested a meeting with the great Mormon Chief Brigham Young. When they met with Brother Brigham and the other leaders of the church, Walker saw the man shown him in his vision. It was Church Patriarch Isaac Morley. Walker told Patriarch Morley as much and informed him that he was to come and live with his people."

"Really? Did he go?" Ammon asked.

"Yup," Sariah said. "Later that year, Isaac Morley led two-hundred forty-four pioneers to the Sanpete Valley, near present day Manti."

"Did Walker tell Morley about Carre-Shinob then?" Ammon asked.

"No, it was about a year later," John went on. "You see, the church had a strong foothold in Utah but was struggling financially. The barter system was alive and well and they even had their own form of paper currency, but they did not have any means of acquiring manufactured goods from the east or doing business with the non-LDS immigrants who stopped in Salt Lake City for supplies."

"What they needed was gold," Sariah said.

"Yes," John continued. "And the Lord did provide. In the spring of 1850, Walker took Patriarch Morley high in the Uintah Mountains to Carre-Shinob. A few weeks later, Morley turned fifty-eight pounds of pure gold over to the church."

"Is that the only time he went to the mine?" Ammon asked.

"No," John answered. "Isaac made one more trip, but then, due to his advancing age, a replacement was agreed upon. In the summer of 1852, a man named Thomas Rhoades took over and made his first of many trips to Carre-Shinob. He brought sixty-two pounds of gold back with him and was gone about two weeks."

"Yeah, Thomas and his son Caleb, who took over for his father when he got too old, are synonymous with the mines, even though they weren't the first whites to go there." Sariah added. "Today, most people call Carre-Shinob the Lost Rhoades Mine."

"If they speak of it at all," John said with disgust. "It never ceases to amaze me how people treat this story like a fairytale. It is absolute, proven fact. The Deseret News recorded Thomas' comings and goings and there are records of every deposit of gold he made in the Deseret Mint, and, yet, the Forest Service denies, up and down, that there is gold in the Uintahs, and mainstream historians dismiss it as some kind of myth. It boggles my mind."

"How much gold did they get?" Ammon asked.

"Over the ensuing decades, father and son retrieved hundreds of pounds," John said.

"People speculate that the gold covering the Angel Moroni, on top of the Salt Lake Temple, came from none other than Carre-Shinob," Sariah added.

"I think that's a reasonable assumption," John said. "Where else would they have gotten it?"

"What happened, you know, with the trips to the mine and stuff? How long did they go there?" Ammon asked.

"The trips eventually stopped," John replied. "Things changed. Chief Walker died, and then his brother, Arapeen, who had the same arrangement with the Indians and the Mormons, died as well. At that point, the

Church's finances had improved enough that the gold was no longer a necessity. Political conditions also changed. The closer they got to the turn of the century, the more control the federal government exercised over the land, eventually closing the High Uintahs to all mineral exploitation. Caleb, getting on in years himself at this point, formed a partnership with a man named F.W.C. Hathenbruck."

"A partnership?" Ammon asked.

"Yes," John continued. "Caleb took Hathenbruck to Carre-Shinob as an act of goodwill and together they petitioned the government for years for the right to legally mine. He said that there was enough gold in there to pay off the national debt. Mind you, *their* national debt was nothing compared to *your* national debt, but still, it amounted to hundreds and hundreds of millions of dollars. You see, we often think of Carre-Shinob as a cave filled with gold, but there is some indication that it is, in fact, a series of manmade chambers cut out of solid gold."

"Huh? Are you kidding?" Ammon asked.

"No," John continued. "People who have claimed to have been there say the walls and pillars appear to be made of solid gold."

"Wow!" exclaimed Ammon.

" 'Wow' is right," replied John. "At any rate, the men's pleas to the government fell on deaf ears. Officially, no one allowed them to return. Caleb eventually died, leaving Hathenbruck the only white man who knew the secret. It is ironic, really: Hathenbruck knew the location of one of the richest sources of gold in the world, and he died poor, selling—That's IT!" John jumped to his feet and shouted.

Everyone in the restaurant stopped talking and stared at him.

"Daddy, will you please sit down and tell us what has excited you so much?" Sariah said gently, but firmly.

"I am sorry." John complied. "I finally realized why the whole sewing machine angle sounded familiar! Hathenbruck died no better than a pauper, trying to make a living selling *sewing machines* door to door![8] I'll bet the old woman's father bought the sewing machine from our good friend, F.W.C, and what we have is most likely his map!"

The map! Ammon had been so engrossed in the story, he had forgotten all about it! His heart began to beat fast. The map! Ammon was now in the possession of a map that could lead him to a vast fortune: a fortune that would simply melt all his money worries away. If he retrieved some of that gold, Sariah would never have to work again. If she needed it, he could afford the best fertility treatment money could buy. He could have all the resources needed to conduct a complete analysis of the glowing stones. All his dreams would come true.

"What are we waiting for?" It was Ammon's turn to jump up from his seat. "Let's go get that gold!"

"And eight dollars and seventy-one cents is your change. Good to see you again, Mr. Byrd," the clerk said, handing John his change.

"Thank you, Emily. It is good to see you, as well," John responded with a smile as he collected the money.

"By the way, you come here too much." Sariah shook her head as they left the Creamery and walked toward their car.

"What? They have really good ice cream, and besides, it is not like I come here *every day*," John said defensively. Sariah chuckled.

"Yeah, they're closed Sundays!" she shot back.

Ammon was not joining in the mirth. John had quickly poured a pro-verbial bucket of cold water onto his enthusiasm regarding the gold. He could not understand John's reaction or the fact that John would not elaborate in the restaurant. For a brief moment, visions of wealth had danced in Ammon's head, before his father-in-law unceremoniously chased them away.

Clicking his seat belt into place, Ammon sought clarification. "Tell me again why we can't go for the gold?"

"I told you, son," John responded patiently, "Carre-Shinob is not meant to be found."

"But why?" Ammon asked, starting the car.

"Well, it is the opinion of many, including myself, that it is hidden and protected by the Indians—held back, if you will—for a very special pur-pose and time," John said reverently, and grew uncharacteristically quiet.

Ammon pulled onto the road and pointed the car toward home. He was confused. There had to be an interesting story behind this comment, and it was quite unlike John not to explain it. After a moment of silence, burst out, "Why? What's the story?"

"Ammon, son, I know you must be worrying about money—every new husband does. I respect that, but…"

"But what?"

"Carre-Shinob is not the answer," John replied. "Countless people since the time of the Spaniards have lost everything searching in vain for the gold. Many have lost their very lives; some…some I have personally known. That is why they say Carre-Shinob is cursed.[9] No one but the Indians, the Keepers of the Yellow Metal, may know of the location."

"Cursed?" Ammon repeated. "Cursed? Doesn't that imply the supernatural? "

"That's exactly what it implies," Sariah added.

"That means either God or the devil is involved. Which one is it?" Ammon asked` skeptically.

"Heavenly Father," Sariah replied.

"Seriously? Why would *He* protect a bunch of gold?" Ammon asked.

"I told you," John joined. "The belief is that the gold is being saved for a special purpose."

"Which is…?" Ammon asked, emphatically.

John did not answer, but rather shot Sariah a worried glance. She gave a slight shrug.

"Come on, John," Ammon continued. "Why are you giving me the run-around? Of course, I want the gold. Who wouldn't? But tell me a good reason to forget about it, and I will forget about it. That's all I want."

"Naturally, Ammon. I apologize. I just have a lot to process right now. I have a wee bit of a history with Carre-Shinob," John gave a short laugh. "It certainly is not like me to spare my listening audience a good story, is it?"

"No," Ammon and Sariah said in unison.

"Fine," John replied. "Guilty as charged. Why *would* Heavenly Father protect a bunch of gold? To make a long story short, He is going to build a really large temple with it."

"Isn't it more like a complex of temples?" Sariah added.

"Yes, that is true," John replied.

"A complex of temples? Seriously? Where will they build it? Salt Lake City?"

"No; Jackson County, Missouri," John said.

"Missouri? The saints got kicked out of Missouri." Ammon said.

"Yes, but it has been foretold that near the second coming of Christ, the Saints will return to Jackson County and build the city of New Jerusalem,"[10] John added.

"Really?" Ammon asked.

Sariah sighed and asked the all too familiar question, "Oh come on Ammon, didn't you ever go to—"

"Primary?" He cut her off. "No, I was out robbing banks, remember?"

"Ha ha, very funny," she retorted. "If you *had* gone to Primary, you would have memorized the tenth Article of Faith: *We believe in the literal gathering of Israel and in the restoration of the Ten Tribes; that Zion (the New Jerusalem) will be built upon the American continent; that Christ will reign personally upon the earth; and, that the earth will be renewed and receive its paradisiacal glory.*"

"Very good. Here I am, all out of gold stars for your forehead," Ammon cooed playfully.

"Cute," Sariah replied. "Anyway, in the center of New Jerusalem, a huge temple, surrounded by a whole bunch of other temple-type buildings, is going to be built."

"Why so many?" Ammon asked.

"To accommodate all of the temple work that needs to be done before, and during, the Millennium," John said. "When Christ returns, he will personally oversee the work."

"So the gold from Carre-Shinob will be used for these temples' construction?" Ammon asked.

"And adornment, yes," John replied. "There are those who believe that is exactly what will happen. Imagine the cost involved in raising such structures. Furthermore, if we are to believe the prophecies regarding the state of the world near the Second Coming, gold will probably be the only means of exchange at that point. Naturally, there are no official statements from the Church regarding the matter, but there are some modern revelations that *hint* as much."

"Oh?"

"Yes, Lorenzo Snow and Spencer W. Kimball both said over the pulpit, years apart, mind you, that the Latter-Day Saints will build the temple in New Jerusalem, with the descendants of the Lamanites playing a special and significant role."[11]

"Couldn't they have meant the Native Americans who joined the church and were just helping alongside everyone else?" Ammon countered.

"It could," John replied. "But why so carefully single them out, while failing to mention the other ethnic groups who have joined the church? Why, President Kimball essentially put the church in a secondary role when he told a group of Lehi's descendants that 'Together you and we shall build in the spectacular city of New Jerusalem the temple to which our Redeemer will come.' "

"You're kidding," said Ammon.

"No," John continued. "I think both brethren were alluding to the fact that, without the treasure contained within the lost mine, the Saints would be unable to build the temple."

"That is why the Native Americans are protecting the gold with help from above," Sariah added.

"And that is why anyone who searches for Carre-Shinob for his own personal gain finds only heartache. That is why, for all intents and purposes, it is cursed," John added.

"Well…I guess the story Sister Henderson told me when I asked her about the map makes more sense now," Ammon said, as he turned the car down their street.

"What was that?" Sariah plied.

"Um…let's see. She said that her father spent many years planning and dreaming of going to the mine. When he finally did, she was a teenager by then, I think. He returned empty-handed. He would not tell his family exactly what had happened, only muttered under his breath about Indians and evil spirits. It drove him mad, really. He spent the rest of his life haunting church history sites around Utah and planning his return for the treasure."

"Sadly, a typical story," John nodded slowly. "In a very real way, I wish you had never found that map, though it is a strange coincidence."

"How's that?" Sariah asked.

"Oh, with all of the excitement right out of the gate, I forgot to tell you two what brought me into town. You see, I was doing some research at the Smithsonian Institute—"

"The Smithsonian?" Sariah interrupted. "You mean they still let you in there?"

"When I use—how should I put this?—an *alias*, they do," John responded with a wink. "In any case, I was in the Smithsonian photography archives when I got a phone call from someone who claimed to be a representative of the Ute nation. He had some questions for me and wanted to know when I was going to be in Utah. Always wanting to stay on good terms with those folks, I dropped what I was doing and headed out here. I met him at the Joseph Smith Memorial Building, in Salt Lake. He was a young fellow by the name of Oquirrh."

"Oquirrh? Like the mountains?" Ammon asked.

"Yes," John replied. "Another Ute name. I told you, they are all around us. Anyway, it did seem strange to me that such a young man would be a tribal elder."

"What did he want?" Sariah asked.

"Oddly enough, he asked me about Carre-Shinob. He seemed to think I knew its location. He said he was trying to protect the tribe's cultural heritage," John said.

"What did you tell him?" Asked Sariah. They were almost to the house.

"I told him what I tell everyone: I do not know where it is. Anyway, not then. People seem to think that the great John Byrd has always had the Lost Rhoades Mine in his back pocket. The whole conversation rather perplexed me. I could not figure out why a Ute Indian, especially a supposed tribal elder, would ask me about Carre-Shinob. I have always suspected they know exactly where it is."

"So, what happened?" Ammon asked. They were pulling into their driveway.

"When I did not tell him what he wanted to know he got frustrated and ended our meeting. Then, coincidentally, I came to see my daughter and found out her husband has acquired what *could* be exactly what he was looking for."

"Could be?" Ammon asked.

"Yes. The map looks authentic and the story certainly fits, but there is something that has been bothering me," John said. "When we get inside, I need to—Wait! Look at your door!"

Ammon's eyes went quickly to the front door. It was ajar and one of the panes of glass was shattered. Ammon saw shards of glass on the ground. A break-in! Someone had broken into their house! His thoughts raced upstairs to the case under his bed and its precious contents.

"We need to call the police!" Sariah said.

Ammon did not heed this advice. Ignoring the tingling sensation at the back of the neck that always warned him of danger, he bolted from the driver's seat and raced into the house. Sariah's shouts of protest echoed distantly in his ears. Bursting through the door, he saw through the front room and into the kitchen. A dark haired man leaned over the counter against the back wall, working on a laptop. Ammon grabbed the fire poker from the hearth and rushed into the kitchen yelling, "Hey pal! You've got exactly two seconds to get out of here!" The man turned around, a Native American in his early twenties. This was not what made Ammon's heart skip a beat as he dropped his makeshift weapon. "Whoa, there, buddy," Ammon said softly, his eyes on the large silver revolver pointed at his chest.

12

"Oquirrh? What are you doing?!" John exclaimed, now standing shoulder to shoulder with Ammon.

Ammon had been so fixated on the stranger and his gun that he had not noticed his father-in–law's arrival. Sariah's startled gasp told him she was hot on her father's heels. Ammon wanted to implore her to leave, but he did not want to take his eyes off the threat in front of him. His military training had taken over and he was analyzing the situation tactically. This man must have followed John to Ammon and Sariah's house and waited for their return. The intruder obviously had the upper hand, but he did not exhibit a command presence. The gunman was clearly nervous, Ammon saw: sweat poured down his face, and he trembled noticeably. Ammon considered his options as the man spoke.

"Hello, John."

At least, Ammon *thought* he heard the man speak. He did not actually see his lips move, and that voice! Something about it confused Ammon. The harsh bass growl did not match the quavering youth in front of him.

The stranger stepped slightly to one side and Ammon understood. The voice came from a laptop on the counter. In a Skype window, Ammon saw a Caucasian male in his mid-thirties with sandy blonde hair. The furrowed skin of his forehead, tight set jaw, and cold stare bespoke deep hatred. Ammon had never seen the man before, but apparently, John had.

"Don," John said slowly, a mixture of horror and amazement in his voice.

"Ah, you still remember me. How touching. I, of course, still remember you," the man on the computer said.

"What—what is the meaning of this, Don?" John said, waving his hand toward the gunman.

"John, John, John," Donald Kress laughed scornfully. "For an intelligent man, you are asking a stupid question. I think it should be quite obvious I mean to avenge myself upon you."

"Avenge yourself?" John responded. "Don, I do not know what happened to you all those years ago, but I warned you not to go looking for Carre-Shinob."

"Warned? Warned!? John, please! Your vague references to Indian curses and gold clad temples hardly constituted a warning!" Donald barked at John. He seemed to be on the verge of losing complete control. "Not to mention the irony of a man who has grown fat on Indian gold himself rendering such a warning. They found me in the mountains, John. They took me prisoner."

"Who took you?" John asked.

"Oh, come on, John. You know perfectly well who: the Keepers of the Yellow Metal, the Yah-keerah. They took me. They would not let me go! For thirteen years, I was their prisoner. Every day, I thought only of Belinda, how our life together would be. When I finally escaped, I found her. She was…she had…" Donald Kress could say no more, his voice choked with a mixture of rage and grief.

"Yes, I know," John said, sympathetically. "I am so sorry. Why don't we—"

"Spare me your sympathy and suggestions!" Donald said, regaining his strained composure. "What you need to do is decide whether or not your lovely daughter is going to join you in death today."

Hearing this, both Ammon and John stepped instinctively between Sariah and the gunman. Their sudden movement made the young man flinch. He looked more terrified than ever.

"Leave her out of this!" John demanded, the color draining from his face.

"Well now, that all depends on how forthcoming you are, doesn't it?" Donald responded.

"What do you mean?" John asked.

"You see John, after I have the pleasure of watching you die, I have something very special in store for our friends, the Yah-keerah."

"What does that have to do with me?" asked John.

"Well, this may or may not surprise you, but I can't seem to find my way back to Carre-Shinob. That being said, if you don't supply me with the information on how to return, your daughter will join you in the afterlife," Donald replied.

"What exactly do you want me to tell you?" John replied. "I don't know where…"

"Don't play games with me, John!" Donald roared. "Tell me where it is! Where is Carre-Shinob?"

"Don, I have told you a hundred times, I don't…" John paused, mid-sentence. An expression of realization swept the worry from his face. He appeared to Ammon as if he were almost relaxed. "Well actually Don, I did recently get my hands on what I believe to be Hathenbruck's map."

"John, don't!" Ammon gasped. "Don't give it to him. I can take this guy!"

"Ah, I see your young friend has caught the gold fever as well." Donald said, with cruel satisfaction. "Be careful, partner," he sneered. "John might send you off into the mountains to your doom. You know; keep the gold for himself. He has been known to do that. Tell me, John; is the map really worth your daughter's life?"

"No, Don. It's not," John said, shooting Ammon an odd look. Ammon thought John was trying to convey a message to him, but he could not tell what it was. "And, if your associate here had looked around a wee bit more, he would have seen that map lying right out in the open. It is over there, on the kitchen table."

"Check it!" Donald ordered. "But keep your eyes on them!"

The gunman backed away from the counter and slowly moved to the table at the side of the kitchen. His eyes darted from one of his captives to the other, like a cornered animal. When he reached the table, he pushed the other paper aside and grabbed the map.

"Boss! I got it!" The man spoke for the first time. He had a strong Native American accent.

"Excellent!" Don said, triumphantly. "Now, get them against the wall over there and then bring the map over and hold it in front of the camera."

With a wave of the gun, the intruder made his intentions clear. John, Ammon, and Sariah backed against the wall opposite the table. Ammon saw John straining to get a look at the map as Oquirrh carried it past him.

"No; that is the screen," Donald said, with surprising patience. "The camera is above. Yes. Right there: good."

With their captor thus occupied, Ammon looked at John and nodded curtly toward the gunman, suggesting they rush him. John gave a quick shake of his head and held up his hand briefly. Ammon got the message. John was advising patience. He was studying the map held in the stranger's unsteady hand and apparently wanted to let the situation play out a little longer.

"Hold it still," Don went on. "Let me see… a little screen capture, and voilà! I have the map! John, isn't it wonderful how much technology has advanced during my thirteen-year vacation? It took the guy at the computer store a little while to get me up to speed, but here we are."

"How fascinating," John muttered, half under his breath.

"Now, go ahead and burn the map," Donald said, as calmly as if he were ordering a pizza.

"NO!" Ammon burst out and started forward. Sariah grasped his arm firmly, stopping him in his tracks.

"Tut, tut, my young friend. I know it doesn't seem like it, but I am actually doing you a favor. As I can attest, the search for Carre-Shinob historically has brought only sorrow. And besides, you won't want to go there when I'm through with it," Donald responded.

As Donald spoke, their captor put the map into his gun hand, pulled a lighter out of his pocket, and started the map on fire. When the flames began to engulf the map, he dropped it to the tile floor. Ammon watched in horror as the flames consumed the solution to all of his problems.

"You know, John, if you had just given my associate here the map at the Joseph Smith building, I could have killed you later myself. Instead, we had to resort to this video chat business. After all, my friend here had to come alone. Your guard certainly would have been up if I had appeared on the front door after all of these years. Then again, I didn't want to miss all the fun either did I? Which reminds me—go ahead Oquirrh; what's the delay?"

"But Boss, we got the map," he responded, his hand trembling more than ever. "We can go back and—"

"First things first, Oquirrh: *kill* John Byrd," Donald said, his former patience with his associate dissipating.

"Boss, I want to obey, but—"

"Kill him, Oquirrh! Now!"

Oquirrh's gun arm lowered, no longer pointed at the three hostages but at the floor. His hand shook violently, the look on his face betraying fear and indecision.

Donald Kress continued to yell at him over the computer. "I saved you from them! You promised to serve me! Shoot John Byrd! Kill him now!"

Ammon made up his mind to charge Oquirrh and disarm him when the look on the gunman's face changed. Deep down, Oquirrh had decided to act. In one swift movement, he swung the gun up, aimed, and fired.

13

Tlahuicle buried himself deeper into his rabbit skin blanket. The icy north wind whipped the walls of the teepee making him feel cold, even by the warmth of the fire. He shivered and stared into the flames. He took some small consolation from the news the Tumpanawach elders had given him a few weeks ago. The Nuche were watchers of the stars and tracked the progression of the great Jack Rabbit. From its position, they knew mid-winter had passed. The time was close at hand when Tlahuicle could continue his mission.

He reached into a nearby woven basket and took a handful of pine nuts. Rolling them in his fingers, he considered the peculiar food. Like the dried fish, deer meat, berries and seeds that the Tumpanawach subsisted on during the winter, the pine nuts were wholesome and sustaining, but simple.

In the royal court in Tenochtitlan, he mused, *we ate the finest foods from the many lands conquered by my people. Even the drink made from the cacao bean that my master drank was so precious, he never used the same golden goblet twice.*[12]

He sighed, and then reproached himself for his ingratitude. The Tumpanawach had been good to him and his men. Their help alone had allowed the foreigners to survive the winter. There were too many of them for one band to shelter, so the royal bearers had dispersed throughout the area to other groups. After a time, many of the men had come to Tlahuicle and asked permission to take wives. He granted permission under the condition they swear an oath to complete their mission when the snows melted. None refrained from taking this oath. Once the treasure was safe, the men would return to live out their lives among these good and generous people.

There had even been maidens belonging to this particular band who had shown such interest in Tlahuicle. Such luxuries, however, were not for him. In his heart, there was only room for one. No matter what woman he looked at, he saw only his beloved Acaxochitl, splendidly arrayed for the great dance. He reached into his blanket and held the golden necklace she had given him on that day. No, there would be no Nuche bride for him. He, unlike his men, would not be returning from the mountains.

Tlahuicle thought of the sacred treasure hidden safely in the nearby woods. He need not have bothered. The members of the band would not seek to steal the gold; the Nuche were not interested in treasure. Other than the small fragments of gold they placed in the bags they wore around their necks, or the occasional golden trinket[13] donned by women, they did not care for the yellow metal. If you could not eat it, and if it did not help you survive the long winter, the Nuche had little use for it.

Tlahuicle returned his gaze to the fire. The children seated in the tee-pee had heaped more fuel onto the flames and were now clamoring for the storyteller to tell another story. The Nuche, young and old alike, loved the stories passed down from generation to generation as well as tales of recent daring deeds. The telling and re-telling of these stories helped to pass the long winter nights.

"All right, all right...." the ancient storyteller relented. "Another tale, I will tell you."

The children immediately settled down and nuzzled up to their parents. A child of six years, one of a large family, leaned against Tlahuicle. This was not unusual: the children of the village were enamored with him. They dotingly called him their 'cousin from the south.' They often followed him around the village, imploring him to recount stories of the great city on the lake in the land where the snow rarely fell. As pleasant as their affection was, his heart ached. It reminded him of the child he and Acaxochitl would never share. Tlahuicle let out a long breath. He had already thought much of her, on this night.

"I will tell you the tale of the god Sinauf and the coming of man into the world,"[14] the narrator continued. A murmur of approval rippled through the teepee.

"Sinauf, who was half man and half wolf, looked out into the world and saw there was no man there. One day, he prepared to take a long journey from his home far to the south into the distant high mountains in the north, the Una-u-quich—these mountains here," he said with a wave of his hand to the east. The children gasped with pleasure.

"Before he left his home, he placed sticks in his magic bag. Once inside, these sticks turned into man. He put many sticks inside and they turned into many people. As he traveled, the people inside the bag made a great noise and commotion. This noise attracted the attention of the animals, especially his brother the coyote. The coyote was very curious and wanted to see these new creatures. The coyote was full of mischief, so he cut a hole in the top of Sinauf's bag, in order to see the people."

Hearing this, the adults muttered their indulgent disapproval. The children looked at each other, wide grins on their faces. Of all the assembled Tumpanawach, the young ones felt the greatest kinship with the coyote and his tricks.

"Being weary from his long journey," the old man continued, "Sinauf did not notice that many of the people leapt from the bag as he walked. These men formed many great tribes along the way.

When he got to Una-u-quich, Sinauf looked out onto the whole world, trying to decide where to place his people. He did not know of his brother's mischief. When he looked inside his bag, he saw only a few people left at the bottom. He removed them from his bag and gave them charge to care for the beautiful mountains. He told them to be brave and strong. Sinauf then returned to his home in the south. This is how the Nuche came into being."

Many of the children were asleep now, and the fire was burning low. Tlahuicle himself felt very sleepy, almost in a trance. He had heard that story many times and it always struck him how different the Nuche and the Aztec creation stories were from each other. The Nuche believed that Sinauf brought them into this land from the south. The Aztecs believed they came into this world in the north, out of a sacred cave with seven different openings, and eventually traveled south.

Tlahuicle laughed sadly. *The southern home I will never see again. The sacred cave, however, I soon will.* With this thought in his mind, he rolled into his blanket and fell asleep.

14

Present Day

The power of the sense of smell to conjure up past memories and, more specifically, strong emotions associated with those memories intrigued Ammon Rogers. The smell of pumpkin pie always reminded him of happy and carefree holidays as a child; freshly cut grass called to mind the exultation of his first touchdown pass; the aroma of auto wax somehow revived the sense of freedom his first car had given him.

It was also an interesting fact that the emotions tied to a certain smell could change, if the triggering event was profound enough. The smell of gun smoke had once evoked the contentment of pheasant hunting alone with his father. After two tours of duty in Iraq, the smell rewoke the fear and odd thrill he felt during his first time in combat. Now, as he considered the prostate figure on his kitchen floor, the smell of gun smoke hanging sharp in the air, Ammon wondered if a new memory would dislodge the old.

It happened so quickly that Ammon struggled to process what had happened. Simultaneously, the revolver discharged like a canon, Sariah screamed, something exploded, and a body hit the floor. Immediately, Ammon had whirled around, certain to see his father-in-law sprawled on the ground behind him. John, however, was standing straight and tall, his daughter next to him. They exchanged a brief, puzzled look. It dawned on Ammon that Oquirrh had fallen. Ammon spun back, expecting the gruesome sight of a man suffering from a self-inflicted gunshot wound. To his surprise, rather than blood, Ammon saw tears.

Oquirrh was not dead, not even wounded, but curled in the fetal position, weeping profoundly. Ammon tore his eyes from the mournful figure and scanned the kitchen, looking for the impact of the bullet. He saw the remains of the laptop on the counter. Where Donald Kress's face once leered at John, there remained only shattered plastic and electronics, the furious shrieks for vengeance replaced by the faint sizzle of fried circuit boards.

The sequence of events finally registered to Ammon: for some reason, Oquirrh had not shot John Byrd, but aimed at the computer instead, collapsing as he silenced his tormentor. Displaying the compassion intrinsic to her gender, Sariah was already at Oquirrh's side.

"No, no—it's okay. You did the right thing. You didn't hurt anyone," she said, placing her hand gently on his shoulder.

With Sariah thus engaged, Ammon moved over next to them and picked up the revolver resting on the floor a few feet away. He made sure the gun was safe and eased the weapon into the back waistband of his pants.

"All is lost! I have disgraced my ancestors—all is lost! I mocked Towats! I have lost everything!" Oquirrh wailed incoherently. The unfortunate man gave no other reply.

After a few moments of trying to console him with no progress, Sariah conceded defeat and stood up. "I think our friend has, uh, checked out," she said, turning to the others.

"Yeah, I think he's boarded the train for La-La Land," Ammon replied.

"This is entirely my fault," John whispered.

"Dad, what is going on here?" Sariah placed her arm around his waist. "Who is…Don?"

"A ghost: a ghost from my past," he responded, almost to himself.

"Dad, you're not making any sense."

"I am sorry, my dear." John sighed, regret splashed across his tired face. "I met Don—Donald Kress—several years ago."

"Thirteen?" Ammon asked, remembering Don's words.

"Yes, it would be about that," John said, stroking his chin. "I met him while giving a lecture on the Aztec/Mayan creation mythology involving seven sacred caves and how it relates to the Book of Mormon and the possible connection to Montezuma's lost treasure."

"Huh?" Ammon asked.

"Well, you see…" John began, his face brightening perceptibly.

"Daddy, that can wait. You were saying?"

"Oh, yes. I am sorry, again," John continued. "Anyway, Don came up to me after my lecture and began to interrogate me for information regarding the location of Carre-Shinob. You see, although I only mentioned it briefly in my lecture, he had heard that I had come into some old Spanish gold. He assumed, incorrectly, that it must have come from the sacred mine. I assured him that I did not know the location of Carre-Shinob, but he would not relent. He begged for any information I had and was so persistent that I finally threw him a bone."

"What did you tell him?" Ammon questioned.

"I told him it was noted that Caleb Rhodes always stopped for provisions in the town of Whiterocks,[15] and that there is some indication that the lost mine is located northwest of Whiterocks Lake. That is all I said as to the location, but I also warned him not to go."

"Like you warned me?" Ammon asked.

"Yes," John continued. "Almost word for word."

"How did he respond to your warning?" Sariah joined.

"He assured me that he only wanted some of the gold in order to be financially secure enough to ask for his girlfriend's hand in marriage, but…" John paused.

"But what?" asked Sariah.

"Well, I am sure he had convinced himself he wanted the gold for his marriage, but I could see the fire of greed burning in his eyes. The thought of such vast wealth has poisoned countless souls."

"So he was captured by the Native Americans who were guarding the mine?" Ammon queried.

"Apparently so, but at the time I had no idea what had befallen him. I expected him to track me down in a few months after an unsuccessful attempt to find the gold. You know, try to hit me up for more information, but that never happened. After not hearing from him for two or so years, I tracked down his girlfriend, Belinda…Belinda Petersen."

"What did she say?" Sariah asked.

"She gave me news that broke my heart," John responded, sadly. "She told me that not long after our meeting, Don had headed off for the High Uintahs in search of the treasure and had never returned."

"Did you suspect at *that* point that he had been captured?" asked Ammon.

"No," John returned. "I had no idea. I simply assumed he lost his way in the wilderness and perished like so many before him. I mean, I knew the legends of the Carre-Shinob being protected by the Indians, but I had never heard any accounts of them actually taking captives."

"That poor girl," Sariah replied. "How was she doing?"

"Oh," replied John. "She was inconsolable for a while. She waited faithfully for a long time for his return. She eventually did marry, but that was years later."

"How do you know that?" Ammon asked.

"I check in on her every few years or so. As you may imagine, I feel some sense of responsibility for Don's disappearance, notwithstanding my warnings. I was genuinely concerned for her welfare, although that has been less of an issue since she wed. She married well and has two beautiful children. I suppose the ulterior motive for my visits has always been to determine if Donald ever resurfaced, but I do really worry about her. Perhaps it is my own sense of guilt. In fact, Ammon, the first time that we met I was in Utah for that very reason."

"I thought you were there to check on Sariah and go fly fishing with Professor Millbarge."

"Those were also on my agenda, but the main reason for coming was to see her. Even though I was excited by your, um, little question, I did not leave for Mexico until I had."

"And she hadn't heard from him at that point?" Sariah asked.

"No," John returned, "but apparently, he is back now and seeking his vengeance: vengeance on me and on the Yah-keerah."

"Fortunately, his plan for you failed," Ammon said, with relief, "but what did he mean when he said he had something special for the Yah-keerah, and where does *this* guy fit into all of this?" Ammon said, nodding in the direction of the still sobbing Oquirrh.

"I do not have the vaguest of ideas," John said with a shrug. "Does he intend to kill the Indians and steal the gold, or blow up the tunnels? Maybe he has nothing planned and this is simply bravado."

"Unfortunately, there's only one way to find out." Ammon said with a wave toward the man curled up on the ground. "And he ain't talkin'."

"So much for a woman's touch," Sariah said, ruefully.

Walking over to examine the wrecked laptop, Ammon suddenly said, "I guess it's not all bad news." He was holding up a lime green toaster with a large hole in it. "Do you think my Aunt Fern will give us another wedding present?"

"I hope not," Sariah responded, earnestly.

"What are we going to do with him?" Ammon said, placing the toaster back on the counter. "Should we call the cops?"

"No. Not yet," John said, contemplatively. "We need to find out what he knows. Let me try a different approach."

John walked into the dining room and grabbed a chair. He came into the kitchen, placed the chair next to the wretched figure, and sat down facing him. After scrutinizing him for a moment, John began, "Oquirrh, I want you to listen to me carefully. Think about your name, son; you are named after a great chief. He led his people with wisdom and skill. You know this, right?"

Oquirrh stopped crying, took a deep breath and nodded weakly. John continued, "Good, good. His name is remembered with honor in the lore of you people, is this not so?"

Oquirrh sat up, looked at John and nodded again, more vigorously.

"Excellent," John said, assuring the stricken man. "Now, Donald Kress is about to do something horrible, something your people will lament for ages to come—something that you will have helped him do."

Oquirrh nodded once more, on the verge of breaking down again.

John quickly continued, "You do not want to let that happen. You do not want to disgrace the name of your noble ancestor. Do you want your people to spit the name Oquirrh rather than to sing it? Tell us what his plans are. We will stop him. We will help you save your honor."

At this, Oquirrh began to wail and lament. "Don't you understand?" he grabbed John's arm. "I gave him the map! It is too late. All is lost!"

15

Travis Stanwick gazed eagerly at the house in the older part of Provo through the bug-splattered windows of his truck. He had done so for the better part of an hour. Could it be that the solution to his riddle, the one that had perplexed him most of his life, had really walked into that house, or was this simply another bitter dead end?

Travis had hardly believed his eyes or his ears when the Indian had come into the rock shop where he worked and wanted to sell the most precious of metals. There was no mistake about it; this was not fool's gold or painted lead. Travis had been around long enough to recognize pure gold when he saw it. The gold was not in bar form, or even a natural-looking nugget. The metal looked sliced off some larger source, like a piece of cheese cut from a wheel at a deli. When Travis saw the gold, the room reeled and he felt a shortness of breath. From the look and sound of the Indian, Travis knew he was a Ute. This gold had to have come from one of the many lost mines, maybe even the big one, Carre-Shinob.

He struggled to gain enough composure to speak, "Yes, well, we do buy gold. Uh, how much ya got there?" he asked, trying to sound nonchalant.

"Don't know."

"Okay, uh, throw it on the scale there," Travis responded. The man complied, and the numbers on the digital scale sprang to life. Two and a third pounds! Sitting on the scale in front of Travis was two and a third pounds of pure gold, possibly from one of the most amazing treasures known to man. He would have to check today's prices, but the gold was easily worth thousands of dollars.

"Whoa buddy, we don't have enough cash to buy all of it," Travis responded truthfully. All the money they had in the cash register and the safe, not to mention the cash value of all the worthless junk in the store, didn't equal the value of that chunk of gold. "We could buy part—

"How 'bout this?" the Ute had interrupted, pulling a smaller chunk of the precious metal out of his pocket.

That did it. After completing the transaction, Travis closed the shop and followed the man. He did not care about this job anymore. This had to be the break he had hoped for all along. It was not hard to trail the man. The Ute was not very aware of his surroundings and seemed rather lost. *Must be his first time off the reservation*, Travis thought.

The Ute met a thirty-something Caucasian man at a computer store, where they stayed for quite a while. Through the window, Travis saw the clerk instructing both men in the use of what a video chat program on two new laptop computers. The stickers were still on the screens.

Once that little bit of business was finished, they took their new laptops and drove to Provo. Travis followed the men in his old beat-up pickup, fantasizing all the way about the treasure that possibly laid at the end of this chase. Their destination was a modest home. Despite its out-of-the-way location, they drove right to the house as though they had been there before.

When the young Ute promptly broke into the house and the other man drove off, Travis figured something interesting was going down. An older man and a young couple arrived a short time later and rushed inside, and Travis knew for sure. What exactly was going down he did not know, but he intended to find out. He had nothing but time.

———

16

"No," John reached over and placed both hands on Oquirrh's shoulders, shaking him firmly. "It is not too late, trust me." He glanced down at the pile of ashes on the floor. "Explain to us this debt you owe him. Tell us his plans. We can stop him. We can help you."

The young Ute took an extremely deep breath and said, "Don't know where to start." Ammon and Sariah gathered around him to listen.

"The beginning is usually the best place," John responded, with a reassuring smile.

"Okay," Oquirrh began. "I was only nine when they brought Don to live with us where the Great Spirit dwells."

"Wait a minute," Sariah interrupted. "You *lived* in Carre-Shinob?"

"Yes, some of my people live in the sacred mine. We are the Yah-keerah."

"Fascinating," John added. "Has it always been so?"

"No, it has only been this way since after the days of Wakara, when the mountains became overrun with the whites. The old chiefs knew where Carre-Shinob was. That was good enough then, but after the whites came, it had to be guarded."

"And so Don was captured by your people?" John asked.

"Yes; the watchers brought him to the chief of the Yah-keerah, Kanosh. He has a gift from Towats; all of the chiefs of the Yah-keerah have this gift. He can look deep into your spirit and see what you most want and what you are willing to do to get it. He can tell other things about people too."

"Did he look into Donald's spirit?" Sariah asked.

"He did. Kanosh saw that there was much greed but also much love. He wanted gold to care for his woman, but he wanted it too much. My people had to keep him. If we had let him go, he would have come back. He would have never stopped. He is not the only one; there are others."

"Others?" questioned Ammon. "Is everyone who gets too close captured?"

"Not everyone. They leave the hunters, fishers, and campers alone. They may get close, but they see nothing. Most seekers for gold can be scared away. The Yah-keerah have always used legend and superstition to protect the treasure, but if a person finds the mine and sees too much, and there is not too much evil in their hearts, keeping them is the only way that pleases Towats. It is not always so, but it happens."

"This Don sure has evil in his heart now," Ammon replied.

"It was not so when he first came to us. In his heart there was much love."

"It is hard to imagine that now," John said rubbing the back of his neck. "What happens if Kanosh finds only evil when he looks into someone's spirit?"

"They are killed. The sacred treasure must be protected. It must be kept for the day that Towats decides to build his great house on the earth," Oquirrh responded, tears welling up in his eyes.

At this, Ammon and John looked at each other in amazement. The legends appeared to be true. The gold was indeed set aside to build the great temple in New Jerusalem, and the Keepers of the Yellow Metal knew it.

"So what happened? How did you…get hooked up with Don?" Sariah asked.

"I was a fool. As a boy, Don would fill the heads of the children with stories of the outside world. The Elders forbade it, but I and another boy, Arapeen, sought him out. We were eager for the stories of cars and music and fancy foods. The two of us grew to hate our lot in life, Arapeen more than I. Still, I wanted to go to the cities where the whites lived. This suited Don just fine, for his bitterness increased as our longing for the world did. The love for his woman faded and his hatred for you and for my people grew. It is hard for love and hate to live under the same roof."

You helped him escape didn't you?" John said.

"Yes," Oquirrh responded, drooping his head. "We made a pact that if Arapeen and I helped him escape and take his revenge, he would show us the ways of the world."

"And so you did," said John.

"Yes. We took some bars of gold with us and escaped. My job was to find you, get the location of Carre-Shinob from you, and then kill you."

"Okay…wait a minute," Ammon interrupted. "Why do you need directions back to a place you just escaped from?"

"Because I don't know how to get back."

"Wait!" Ammon said scratching his head. "Now I'm really lost."

"More so than usual?" Sariah asked, elbowing him gently.

"Ha ha, very funny," Ammon responded. "No, I mean, really, how do you not know where you were?"

"Part of my people live in the sacred caves and roamed only the hills nearby. Another part of my people lives in a village down the mountain and bring supplies only close to Carre-Shinob, but they do not know the entrance."

"Huh?" responded Ammon. "That doesn't make sense."

"No, it is brilliant actually," John said, admiringly. "It is a perfect scheme for protecting the mine. Since they were not exactly sure where it was, no one from the outside tribe could divulge the secret or be followed there. On the other hand, if someone from the inside tribe left, there is a good chance they would not be able to find their way back. The forests and canyons of the Uintahs are like a maze."

"It is true. I was brought there when I was very little, chosen by my parents to serve where the Great Spirit dwells. I had never been to the outside world since. When we escaped, we had to follow a supply train back to the village. There was no other way we could have made it. Since they only travel by night, to avoid notice, we really don't know the way back."

"I guess that does make sense," Ammon admitted.

"Yes, and there's also the way that people sometimes have *help* forgetting the way back," Sariah added.

"What on earth does that mean?" Ammon asked.

"What my well-educated daughter is referring to is the story of Pete Miller, a grizzled old prospector who, very probably, found Carre-Shinob," John said, a little proudly.

"He did?" asked Ammon.

"Yeah," Sariah responded. "He found the mine by accident one day and even retrieved a small quantity of gold and jewels, which he showed to some friends later."[16]

"Why didn't he go back for more?" Ammon asked.

"He tried," Sariah continued. "The trouble was, he couldn't find his way back, no matter how hard he looked."

"His friends thought he had had a stroke," John added. "He, however, was convinced, until the day he died, that the knowledge had been *taken* from him by a higher power."

"His memory had been wiped clean by the wrath of Towats," Sariah said, ominously.

"I don't get it. Why allow him to find it and then leave?" Ammon snorted. "Was it the Yah-keerah's day off or something?"

"No," Oquirrh replied. "This story is well known among my people. The old man was allowed to do what he did because it was the will of Towats."

"Why the inconsistency?" Ammon asked, scratching his head. "Why are some allowed to go and others held hostage, while still others are killed? I don't understand."

"It is not always for man to understand the ways of Towats," Oquirrh replied, with a shrug.

"That is true," John agreed. "Needless to say there is a precedent for people not being able to find their way back to Carre-Shinob. It is not at all surprising that Donald needs the map."

After a moment of silence, Ammon asked, "Oquirrh, what is Don going to do to the Yah-keerah? He said he had something special in store for them."

The young Ute shook his head sadly and then responded, "I do not understand what he is doing. After we escaped, he stole something from a hospital in Salt Lake City. He said that it would kill the Yah-keerah and make it so no other people could go to the mine and use the gold for a long, long time."

"What did he steal, germs?" Sariah asked.

"No, wait," Ammon interjected. "What did it look like? The thing Don stole?"

"It was a metal case with little…cans inside," Oquirrh responded.

"Did the case have any words on it?" asked Ammon.

"Yes," he responded, slowly. "I can't remember exactly, but it had a C and an S and some numbers."

"CS 137!" Ammon exclaimed.

"I think so."

"Oh man! He's going to hit the Yah-keerah with a dirty bomb!" Ammon cried.

"What is a dirty bomb?" John and Sariah asked, simultaneously.

"Well, a dirty bomb is—wait a minute," Ammon said, with a faint grin forming on his face.

"What?" John asked.

"I just gotta savor this moment," Ammon responded, almost laughing now.

"What?!" Sariah practically yelled.

"I think this is the first time since I've known you guys that *I* have had to explain some important point to you all. It feels good, for a change," Ammon responded, with a chuckle.

John started to chuckle as well. Sariah, however, looked at Ammon keenly and said, "Cute. Now, please tell us what a dirty bomb is, exactly, or I'll put one under your pillow tonight."

"Okay, okay; rob me of my triumph, if you must," Ammon smiled. "Anyway, dirty bombs are very dangerous. We always worried about them, in Iraq."

"Are they really big or something?" Sariah asked.

"No," Ammon replied. "It fact, they can be rather small. A dirty bomb is made of conventional explosives, something like C4 or dynamite or even black powder. What makes them dangerous is that, wrapped around the bomb, is some sort of highly radioactive or 'dirty' material."

"Does the explosion trigger a nuclear reaction?" John asked.

"No," Ammon responded, "but what it does do is spread the radioactive junk all over the place. If the initial blast does not kill the people nearby, the radiation will. And depending on the level of radiation, it will kill them sooner rather than later."

"Oh no!" Sariah gasped.

"That's not the worst part," Ammon continued. "Depending on the extent of the contamination, the affected area could be rendered uninhabitable for hundreds of years."

"What would the effects of such a bomb be inside of an enclosed space like Carre-Shinob?" John asked stroking his chin.

"Catastrophic," Ammon replied, "if the nuclear material is potent enough. There is no wind to dissipate the radiation. It would all stay right there. You seriously wouldn't want to step foot in there or remove anything from it for a very long time."

"What is CS 137?" Sariah asked.

"Cesium-137," Ammon replied. "It's used for cancer treatments. It makes perfect sense that Don stole it from a hospital."

"Is it potent enough to do what you have described?" John asked.

"Oh yeah," Ammon responded, "if he has enough of it—and from Oquirrh's description, it sounds like he does. Don is definitely going to roast Carre-Shinob!"

"It is the perfect revenge," John added. "Not only will he destroy the people who held him captive, but he will also make it so the gold cannot be used for its holy purpose!"

Hearing this Oquirrh began to wail and lament anew. "I have betrayed Towats! All is lost! All is lost!"

"We've got to do something! Should we call the police or FBI or something?" Sariah asked.

"And tell them what?" John said grimly. "That a man who was declared dead years ago has returned and intends to blow up a mine no one believes exists?"

"He's right," Ammon agreed. "They won't believe us."

"Well, we're going to have to stop him ourselves then, aren't we?" Sariah said, stamping her foot.

"But how?" Ammon asked. "He's got the map *and* a head start."

"Oh," began John slyly. "It is true that he has a head start, but I would not worry about the map."

"Why?" the three young people said at once.

"Because," John replied with a smile, "that map is not going to lead Don anywhere."

17

"Come again?" Ammon asked, flatly.

"Donald will not find Carre-Shinob using that map," John reiterated.

"Why not?" Ammon asked.

"It is a fake," John said confidently. "It was worth no more whole than it is as a pile of ashes."

"A fake?" Ammon, Sariah, and Oquirrh said in unison.

"Yes."

"But Daddy, you said…" Sariah paused, trying to find the right words.

"I said it looked promising," John said. "However, something about the map was bothering me the whole time we were at the ice cream parlor. I could not put my finger on it. I wanted to carefully examine it when we got home, but, well…you know."

"Then how can you be so sure?" Sariah asked.

"I managed to get a decent look at the map as Oquirrh walked past me and while he was holding it up to the computer, and confirmed what bothered me," John replied.

"Which was?—" Sariah asked.

"The symbols were wrong," said John.

"Symbols?" Ammon asked.

"Yes," John continued. "You see, the Spanish and the prospectors who followed them used a unique set of symbols on their maps. They also carved these symbols into trees and rocks in the vicinity of their mines and claims. Now, unlike the symbols on modern maps or the road signs we are all familiar with, these symbols were not intended to aid the viewer."

"What, then?" Ammon asked.

"They were a type of secret code that held important meanings for the initiated and brought confusion and misdirection to the uninvited.[17] Sometimes these symbols even warned of, or lead to, death by pitfall or other trap. This, of course, depended on how they were interpreted," answered John.

"Wow," Ammon said. "That's a bit extreme."

"When it comes to gold," Sariah added, "people don't mess around."

"If these symbols are shrouded in so much mystery, how do we know what they mean?" asked Ammon.

"Well, they were used for long enough and by enough people that they coalesced into recognizable archetypes. Although there was always variation, we know, more or less, the meaning of many of the old Spanish Symbols."

"And the symbols on my map were wrong?" inquired Ammon.

"The ones I could see, yes," John responded. "For instance, the symbol of the turtle."

"Oh, yeah!" Ammon interjected. "I saw that one. That is a map symbol. I thought it meant there were lots of turtles in the mountains."

"No," John added. "It is a map symbol, all right, and an important one at that. The position of the head, legs and tail reveal important clues, including a direction to the mine."

"So, what was wrong with my turtle?" Ammon asked.

John was about to answer when Sariah said with a giggle, "I must admit that is a phrase I never expected to hear you say."

"Life with me is certainly full of surprises," Ammon shook his head. "Anyway, John… my turtle?"

"Yes, well…" John continued, "your turtle had no tail. No treasure hunter worth his salt would make such an omission, let alone someone with Rhodes' or Hathenbruck's experience. A turtle with no tail is a useless symbol, and men such as this did not waste their time with needless things. And then there was this symbol…"

John reached for a stack of sticky notes and a pencil on the counter. Peeling off the top paper, Sariah's shopping list, John jibed, "Sugar-frosted Cocoa Puffs? Do you really eat such things?"

"I am making up for the deprivation I suffered as a child," Sariah returned.

Chuckling to himself, John drew a symbol that looked like an upper case T with a small circle attached to the bottom post.

"Yes," Ammon said nodding. "I remember seeing a symbol like, that only it—"

"Looked like this?" John said turning the paper upside-down so the circle was now on top.

"Yeah, yeah," Ammon affirmed. "That's it."

"What does that mean?" Sariah asked.

"When it is oriented like this," John said, turning the symbol back, "it means 'treasure buried deep below.' "

John turned the paper so the symbol appeared as it had on the map. "When it looks like this, the symbol becomes nonsense. You cannot bury treasure high above."

"Unless it is talking about building up treasures in heaven," Sariah postulated.

"I doubt it," John responded shaking his head. "Hardcore treasure hunters frequently neglect such spiritual matters. No, the symbol is just plain wrong."

"Maybe whoever made the map simply made a mistake?" Reasoned Ammon.

"No," John said. "Assuming that this is Hathenbruck's map, or at least a copy of it, I really do not think he would commit such errors."

Ammon thought a moment and asked, "So, you really think the map's a fake?"

"Actually, fake is probably the wrong term for it. I think that map was meant as a decoy." John responded.

"Decoy?" Sariah asked.

"Yes," John continued. "I think someone, presumably the old woman's father, prepared this map as a decoy to throw off would-be claim jumpers. He mixed up the symbols as a kind of inside joke or even as a reminder for himself. The age of the paper lends credence to my theory."

"Age of the paper?" Ammon repeated.

""Yes," John replied. "I am no document expert, but I know enough to tell the difference between thirty-year-old paper and hundred-year-old paper."

"Why would he do that?" asked Ammon.

"I told you," John responded, "treasure hunters are very paranoid. He wanted to draw attention *to* the phony map and *away* from the thing that revealed the true location of Carre-Shinob."

"Which is?" Ammon asked.

"That document right over there," John pointed to the kitchen table.

Ammon spun around and saw the other document he found in the lid of the sewing machine. The discovery of the map and the ensuing recent events had eclipsed the memory of the second paper, covered with lines and words.

Walking over and retrieving the paper, Ammon asked, "This thing will lead us to Carre-Shinob?"

"That is correct," John replied. "It is my theory that using the original Hathenbruck map, the father of the old woman made this puzzle, or whatever it is, detailing the location of the mine, then fabricated a decoy map, and hid or disposed of the original map. He was either a genius or insane, or both."

"What do you mean, Dad?"

"Well, he might have been paranoid and driven to madness by longing for the gold, but his plan certainly worked. Donald Kress is now racing off to the High Uintahs with a decoy map, and we have the true location of the treasure, providing we can interpret it. I looked at it briefly before. It looked like a mess of numbers, lines and riddles. It appears to be some kind of coordinates. That being said, it does not resemble any latitude-longitude coordinate system I have ever seen."

Ammon looked at the paper in his hands as if for the first time. The lines and numbers that comprised the center of the document did look familiar to him and after a moment's reflection, he realized why.

$$12 \text{ T } 05\_65\_\_.\_\_\text{ ME}$$
$$\_51\_1\_\_.\_\_\text{ MN}$$

He started to laugh as it all became clear to him, "Could it really be? Two times in one day?"

"What two times?" Sariah asked.

"Could it be that I know something you two don't, twice in one…"

"Ahem!" Sariah cleared her throat loudly, cutting him off. Glancing at her, Ammon could tell by the squint in her eyes and the hand resting on her hip that he had better not finish that sentence.

"Uh…anyway John, you're right," Ammon continued, sheepishly. "They are coordinates…They're UTM coordinates."

"UTM?" John responded.

"Yeah," Ammon said, nodding. "It stands for Universal Transverse Mercator. It is a mapping method developed shortly after World War II."

"How does it work?" asked Sariah.

"Well…instead of using latitude and longitude, degrees, seconds and all that stuff, the UTM system divides the world into sixty zones. The T number here expresses the zone. I'm pretty sure that 12 T is the zone where Utah sits," Ammon said, holding out the paper so the others could see it.

"What do the other numbers mean?" John asked.

"They are how you find something inside the zone," Ammon continued. "This top set of numbers here, next to the T number, is how many meters east your subject is from a fixed line inside the zone. The ME stands for meters east."

"And MN stands for meters north?" John surmised.

"Yup," responded Ammon.

"North of what?" Sariah asked.

"The Equator," replied Ammon. "That bottom number indicates how many meters north of the Equator your subject is. UTM is not a bad system. It's fairly precise."

"I've never heard of it," John admitted.

"Not too many people have," Ammon responded. "I learned about it in Army map school. You can set Google Earth or most GPS units to run UTM coordinates, but it is by no means the default setting."

"What are those lines, or blank spaces?" asked Sariah. "Are they part of the system, too?"

"No, there should be numbers there," Ammon responded. "Both top and bottom numbers should have seven digits. Man! He has even calculated the coordinates to the hundredth meter for added accuracy. This guy wasn't messing around."

"Why would he be that precise?" Sariah asked. "We're looking for a big cave, right?"

"No," John added. "He would need to be quite precise. It is said that if you do not know exactly where the opening is, you could walk right past it and not even notice."

"How do we use the coordinates with all of the missing numbers?" asked Sariah.

"That is where these words come in, I assume," John said. Along the edges of the paper were handwritten groups of words. With one exception, each word group had a thin line leading from it to a different missing number or short sequence of numbers.

"These are most likely riddles or clues devised by the old man," hazarded John. "This was another way of protecting his secret."

"Solve the riddle, get a number," Ammon said, turning the paper back around and scrutinizing the writing.

"Get all the numbers," Sariah joined, "find Carre-Shinob."

"That is correct," John replied, nodding gravely.

"Which means we can go there and warn the Yah-keerah," said Sariah.

"Yes," said John.

"Well, don't just stand there, Ammon," Sariah said, stamping her foot. "Tell us the first clue!"

18

Ammon Rogers had never been a morning person, but during his two tours of duty in Iraq, he grew to hate the wee hours of the morning. It was one thing to have to get up early for football practice or a hunting trip; it was quite another thing to wake up early to be shot at, or possibly blown to bits. His detest of early wake-ups had faded a bit since he came home, but here he was again, watching the sunrise, his heart filled with fear and uncertainty.

He had to admit that speeding north on I-15 with the sun peeking over the mountains was exhilarating and beautiful. Something else pleased him, as well. A change had come over Sariah. As she sat next to him in their car, Ammon saw the old fire returned to her eyes. This new adventure, fraught with danger as it was, had set her spirits soaring again.

Ammon laughed to himself. His wife had been ready to charge off that evening and find Carre-Shinob all by herself, if need be. It reminded Ammon of a time when the unarmed Sariah was ready to take on a group of trigger-happy kidnappers in order to rescue her father. Fortunately, once again, cooler heads had prevailed. John had a plan.

"Sariah, my dear," John had said. "It is getting too late in the day. We need to make a plan of attack, rest, and prepare."

Sariah responded angrily, "We don't have time for this! Donald already has a head start!"

"We have time," John replied. "The decoy map will slow him down enough, and besides, running off half-cocked will do us no good."

"About Don and his map," Ammon asked. "Why do we even need to go after him? With the bogus map, will he even be able to find the mine?"

"You have a point there, son," John responded. "The trouble is we do not know how far off-course the map will take him. From what I remember, it might put him in the ballpark."

"That is assuming he doesn't realize right off the bat that it's a fake," Sariah put in.

"True," John continued. "Donald is well-versed in mining lore. He might recognize the incorrect symbols as well. My worry is if he can get close to Carre-Shinob by using the map or some other means, his Ute companion will be able to take him the rest of the way there."

"I didn't think about that," Ammon admitted. "That's possible."

"It is very possible," John said gravely. "That is why Oquirrh and I are going to attempt the same thing."

"What?" Sariah cried.

"I am sorry, my dear," John replied, "but I really think it would be best to divide our efforts. Using what I know, or think I know, about Carre-Shinob, I will try to get our friend here close. With any luck, he will be able to recognize something."

"But—" Sariah began to protest.

John cut her off. "Meanwhile, you and Ammon try to decipher the clues and find the coordinates. By working at this problem from different ends, we increase our chances for success."

"But Daddy," Sariah continued to protest. "Why don't we all work on the riddles together? You said yourself this would lead us to the mine."

"Theoretically," John countered. "Who is to say, however, that we would even be able to figure it all out? It sounds like the old man was half-mad when he devised his plan. No, we cannot put all of our eggs in one basket like that. There is too much riding on this."

Sariah continued her protests, but John would hear nothing of it. "This really is the best plan. I need to get a few supplies together; then Oquirrh and I are going to try to make it as far as Roosevelt tonight."

"Roosevelt? Tonight?" Sariah cried.

"Yes," John replied. "I need to get to the Frontier Motel as soon as possible."

"The Frontier Motel?" Ammon repeated. "What's there?"

"The Frontier Motel and Café is a kind of Mecca for local treasure hunters.[18] I know a man who frequents that establishment who might be able to assist us. We will spend the night there and get an early start for the mountains."

"Why don't we contact officials from the Ute nation and warn them?" Ammon asked.

"That is problematic," John replied. "They do not officially acknowledge the existence of Carre-Shinob and, even if they believed us, I doubt they could get a message to them any faster than we could."

"But—but—" Sariah sputtered.

"No buts," John replied. "Now daughter, will you please trust me? This really is the best way."

"Dad," Sariah said, her voice catching in her throat. "What if we can't solve these riddles without you?"

John walked over to his daughter and kissed her on the forehead. "My dear, if memory serves, I was in a coma when you and Ammon recovered the lost stones."

"That doesn't count," Sariah protested. "You led us practically right up to the door."

"Daughter," John replied. "I have no doubt whatsoever that if you trust yourselves, each other, and the Lord, you will be successful in this endeavor, as well."

When John and Oquirrh were leaving, Ammon took his father-in-law aside and expressed his concern. "John, do you really think you can trust this guy? He could have very easily killed you just a few hours ago. I'm worried about you running off with him."

"Trust me, son," John replied. "That same thought has crossed my mind, but my heart tells me I can trust him. I believe he truly wants to redeem himself for betraying his people."

"Well…okay. I'd feel better though if you took this," Ammon said, reaching into the back waistband of his pants and retrieving the gun that had almost been the means of John's demise.

"You keep it," John replied. "To be honest with you, I am not that fond of guns. Besides, you might need it at some point, to protect yourself from Sariah."

After the final preparations for departure, John hugged his daughter, shook Ammon's hand, and drove away with Oquirrh at his side. After they drove around the bend and disappeared from sight, Ammon had a sinking feeling in the pit of his stomach. John had so skillfully lead the three of them in the past. Ammon shared his wife's anxiety over not having him with them. It was now all up to Ammon and Sariah.

Brushing a tear from her cheek, Sariah turned to Ammon. "Let's get started."

"Okay," Ammon replied. "But, where do we even start? I was looking at some of the riddles, and they don't even make sense."

"Well, I was thinking," Sariah replied as they walked back into their house. "You said Sister Henderson's father spent the rest of his life hanging around church history sites, right?"

"Yes."

"It might stand to reason, then," she continued, "that these riddles would have something to do with church history. If we view the riddles through that lens, they might make more sense."

"That sounds good. Let's take a crack at it!"

Ammon and Sariah sat down at their kitchen table and each held a side of the document. After reading the different riddles, Sariah pointed to a particular paragraph in the upper left hand corner. "Look at this one: it's bigger and bolder, and doesn't have a connecting line to a blank spot. Maybe this one is a key to the rest."

"Who knows?" Ammon had replied. "Reading this stuff, I think this guy was nuts. Listen:"

The Sphynx is drowsy,
Her wings are furled
Her ear is heavy,
She broods on the world:
Who'll tell me her secret
The ages have kept?

I awaited the Seer,

While they slumbered and slept.

"A sphinx?" Ammon had said with exasperation. "What does an ancient Egyptian monument have to do with church history?"

"Nothing as far as I know, except for the biblical and Pearl of Great Price references to Egypt. The word *seer* though: that is one of the titles given to a prophet."

"Yeah, but are we talking ancient or modern prophets? Ancient Egypt would relate better to ancient prophets, but church history sites around Utah would relate better to the latter -day variety."

Ammon and Sariah sat in silence, each racking their respective brains. After ten minutes, Sariah said, dejectedly, "I really can't think of any connection a latter-day prophet had to the Sphinx."

"Oh come on, didn't you ever go to Primary?" Ammon asked jokingly, trying to lighten the mood.

"Yeah, but it's not helping me on this one."

"Well…what do we do now?"

At this moment, Ammon felt even lower. Finances were so tight that they could only afford necessities. Having grown up in far-off unconnected places, Sariah did not consider the internet and smart phones necessities. Ammon wished they had them now. A quick online search might give them something to go on.

Sariah sighed and replied, "You're not going to like it, but I think I know someone who can help us."

"Who? Professor Millbarge?" Ammon responded. Professor Millbarge had been Ammon's Book of Mormon Professor. He had first introduced Ammon to John Byrd, and he remained a close family friend.

"No, not Millbarge."

"Oh no: you don't mean—"

"Kevin—yes," Sariah had responded.

"Okay, whatever." Ammon sighed resignedly. "If you think he can help."

Sariah placed her phone on the table in speaker mode and hit the speed dial. The phone rang three times before a nasally male voice answered, "Sariah! What a pleasant surprise. Tell me this phone call means that you have finally left that no-good husband of yours?"

———————

19

Rounding the Point of the Mountain on I-15, Ammon saw the sun hitting the tops of the Oquirrh Mountains. *Oquirrh*, Ammon mused, *the same name as John's accidental companion. I hope he knows what he is doing.* As for Ammon and Sariah, they were now about thirty minutes away from their destination: a place that, before last night, Ammon had never heard of. Thinking of the phone conversation that set them on this path, Ammon cringed.

Kevin Mitchell worked with Sariah at the BYU library. He was an overweight, thirty-something computer gamer who, although he had probably never been on a date in his whole life, constantly flirted with Sariah and all of his other female co-workers. While he put off the other women at the library, Sariah found him oddly endearing, like a geeky little brother, and actually formed a friendship with him. Ammon had known why she had called him for help, right away. The guy was a whiz on the internet and had the makings of a first rate researcher if he did not fritter away his life playing World of Warcraft. Sariah found him amusing and harmless. Ammon did not.

"I can hear you, Kevin," Ammon responded to his crack about Sariah leaving him. "We're on speaker phone. You shouldn't say stuff like that. I'm having a bad flare up of battle-induced Post Traumatic Stress Disorder today. I could snap at any time."

Sariah elbowed Ammon and laughingly mouthed the word "Stop!"

"Oh…Oh…Sorry," Kevin responded, sheepishly. "Then to what do I owe the pleasure?"

"What are you doing?" Sariah had asked.

"My guild and I are preparing to go on a raid the Dragonmaw Fortress."

Hearing Kevin's response, Ammon said under his breath, "Did you really have to ask?" Sariah had elbowed him again.

"Why do you ask?" Kevin responded.

"Well…if you're not too busy, I need your help," Sariah said.

"Anything for you; how may I be of service?"

At this reply, Ammon rolled his eyes.

"Great, thanks. Ammon and I are on a kind of a…scavenger hunt, and we need to solve a riddle. Do you think that you could use your *unparalleled* internet skills and see if this riddle is associated to any location here in Utah?"

"Flattery will get you everywhere," Kevin responded, proudly. "Let me get a search engine up." There was a pause. ""Okay, go ahead and tell me the riddle."

Sariah read the riddle to him. After a few moments Kevin responded, "Hmmm, interesting. Looks like that is a poem written by… Ralph Waldo Emerson. Don't see any association with Utah, however."

Sariah looked at Ammon and frowned. Kevin continued, "Let me try searching sphinx and seer or maybe prophet…okay, we got some book called the "Sphinx Prophet" by a guy named Dan Schmidt…nothing to do with church history though."

"Why don't we get more specific?" Sariah responded. "Try some of the names of the modern prophets."

"Which one?" Kevin had asked.

"Well… the poem says '*Who'll tell me her secret the ages have kept? I awaited the seer while they slumbered and slept*'," Sariah returned.

"Could that somehow be referring to the Restoration of the Gospel?" Ammon postulated.

"I think so!" Sariah replied excitedly. "Kevin, try Joseph Smith."

"Okay, just a sec—hold on!" Kevin replied. "This is interesting."

"What?" Ammon and Sariah both burst out.

"Well, it seems that in Salt Lake City there is a place called Gilgal Garden."

"Okay. And?" Sariah said.

"And…Gilgal Garden contains, among other interesting things, a two ton stone Sphinx with—you're gonna love this—the face of Joseph Smith carved on it![19] Furthermore, that poem of yours is engraved on a flat stone right next to it." Kevin replied proudly.

Ammon and Sariah looked at each other in amazement. This had to be the place. A sphinx with Joseph Smith's face was strange enough somehow to fit perfectly.

"Great, Kevin!" Sariah affirmed. "I think that is exactly what we are looking for. I knew you were the right man for the job."

"Oh, Sariah…stop it," Kevin replied. Ammon ground his teeth.

"Kevin?"

"Yes?"

"Is there any way I could call you tomorrow morning, you know, if we need some more help?" Sariah inquired.

"I don't know. I sleep kinda late…"

"Oh, come on. We'll buy you a new Spock T-shirt."

"All right. I'll leave my phone by my bed."

"Thanks. I owe you one," Sariah responded, terminating the call.

"You know, we could have looked that up ourselves," Ammon had replied, folding his arms.

"There, don't be jealous," Sariah placated him. "I didn't realize it was going to be that easy. Then again, who is to say this is even the solution to the riddle? I don't know; it's good to have him on board, especially when we are out in the field tomorrow. Come on; let's get to bed. We've got to get an early start in the morning."

Ammon exited I-15 and merged their car onto eastbound I-80.

"Are you sure this is the right way?" he asked.

"That's what Google maps says," Sariah replied, cheerfully.

She really is enjoying this little adventure! Ammon thought. Apprehension filled him, not necessarily because of the uncertainty of the journey ahead, but because of what he had left behind.

"Do you really think the glowing stones will be okay?" Ammon asked, for the third time. The trauma of having his home invaded the day before was still fresh. He worried that someone else would break in and steal his most precious earthly possession.

"I've told you, your hiding place inside the furnace vent is brilliant. If someone breaks in, they are definitely not going to look in there," Sariah replied.

Ammon did not know what he would do if anything were to happen to the stones. It was his greatest wish to find out what made them tick. What amazing new energy sources would he find? If only he had the money. In spite of John's warnings and explanation regarding the gold's special destiny, Ammon found himself longing for what lay at the end of their journey. *Would it really hamper the building of the temple in Jackson County if I kept a little gold? It would be for a worthy cause.*

"Take this next exit and head north on Seventh East," Sariah instructed. "Keep heading north for a while and watch for Fifth South."

Thinking again of Jackson County reminded him of a question that had been bothering him. After framing his words carefully he said, "Sariah, something's been bugging me."

"How stunningly beautiful I am?" Sariah replied, with a smile.

"No, that's a good thing." He smiled at her. "It's the whole Jackson County thing."

"Oh? What about it?"

"Well, you and your dad said the big temple is going to be built in New Jerusalem and that Christ himself would come there."

"Yeah, so?"

"What I was wondering was, why it didn't happen when the Saints were there in the first place?"

"It was supposed to," Sariah replied matter-of-factly.

"It was?"

"Yeah," Sariah continued. "In Doctrine and Covenants 84:5, the Saints at that time were told, 'This generation shall not pass away until an house shall be built unto the Lord."

"Then why didn't it happen? Why were they kicked out?

"Simply? It was because the Saints became wicked."[20]

"Really?" Ammon replied.

"Yup. I mean, there wasn't mass apostasy or anything like that, just a lot of envy, strife, and contention."

"Ouch."

"For sure. The Lord's plans couldn't work in conditions like that and so He told the Saints in Doctrine and Covenants 105:9: *Therefore, in consequence of the transgressions of my people, it is expedient in me that mine elders should wait for a little season for the redemption of Zion.*"

"How is it that you can't remember where the car keys are but you have all of these scriptures memorized?" Ammon asked, shaking his head and smiling.

"Who's my father?"

"Good point," Ammon replied, laughing now.

"Keep your eyes open; Fifth South should be coming up soon," Sariah warned, laughing as well.

"Okay," Ammon replied and then, after a moment, continued: "You know, that story begs a very interesting point."

"Which is?"

"The implication in that story is that, had the Saints not fallen into transgression, the Second Coming of Christ would have already happened."

"I guess it does," Sariah said, thoughtfully. "I've never thought of it like that before."

"If that is truly the case, we humans underestimate the consequences of our actions and our power to shape the future."

"Here's the real kicker," Sariah added. "Heavenly Father knew when He originally made that prophecy regarding the temple that it wasn't going to happen till later, and yet he still said it. Wrap your mind around that."

Ammon whistled and said, "That's way too deep a thought for a kid who never went to Primary."

"Oh, here it is. Turn right now."

Ammon complied and turned onto the street.

"It should be mid-block on the north side of the street. Just park any-where," Sariah instructed.

Ammon pulled into the first available spot. They exited the car and looked around.

"Where is it?" Ammon said. "I don't see any kind of a park. All I see are houses."

"The address is right. It should be right here," Sariah said. "Wait! Look between those two houses: an iron gate."

They walked toward the gate and a sign came into view. It read, *Gilgal Garden*, and listed the hours of operation.

"To steal a famous line, *This is the right place*," Sariah said.

"Brigham Young, right?"

"Very good," Sariah said, with mock pride.

"Never went to Primary, huh?"

Ammon and Sariah entered the gate and walked down a long tree lined path between two houses. Ammon had a hard time imagining a large sculpture garden simply tucked behind these ordinary residences, but that was exactly the case. After a short walk, Gilgal Gardens sprang into view, and as Ammon looked around, he decided he had never seen a stranger place.

20

Travis Stanwick pulled onto the residential street just in time to see the man and woman he was following disappear between two houses. The paper, which he believed contained his hopes and dreams, was still in the woman's hands. He breathed a sigh of relief. *I haven't lost them. I still have a chance*, he thought. It was a chance Travis thought he had lost.

While he watched the house in Provo, the Ute entered, then three others. Travis found himself fantasizing about the gold. This was not new for him: in fact, he had spent most of his life doing so. This time, however, it had seemed so close he could touch it. One or more of the people inside that house knew where it was.

At one point during his vigil, Travis thought he heard a gunshot, but he could not be sure. Was someone else trying to gain the knowledge he so desperately sought? Travis fought the urge to grab his own gun and charge into the house.

No, he told himself. *It will be better to wait, watch, and follow.* Following the suspicious noise, the house was still. Travis perceived no movement of any kind. Eventually, it had gotten late and, despite his best efforts, he fell asleep. While he slept, Travis dreamt of his mother. She had said nothing to him but stood in front of him shaking her head slowly, her face awash with disappointment. Travis tried to tell her that it was all right and that his search would soon be over, but he could not utter the words.

Travis was jolted awake, when the sprinklers in front of the house kicked on at 5:30 and showered him through the open window of his truck. He tried to shake the all-too-familiar look on his mother's face from his mind as he rolled up the window. After he rubbed the sleep from his eyes, Travis saw something that made his blood run cold: one of the vehicles parked in front of the house—the Land Rover—was gone.

What have I done? They are gone and so is my chance! he thought, full of self-loathing.

Flooded with panic, Travis reached for his keys and was about to fire up his truck when he paused. The young couple he had seen the night before were walking out the front door and heading for the car parked in the driveway. The man kept looking back at the house, as if he was worried about something he was leaving behind. Travis wondered momentarily what it could be, but was more interested in what the woman was carrying in her hand. It was a rather old looking piece of paper.

A map! He had thought. *That has to be a treasure map! They are going after the gold!* Travis was now completely disinterested in the whereabouts of the older man and the Indian. He knew what he needed to do. He still had a chance.

When the couple did not exit I-15 and go up Provo Canyon towards the Uintahs, he was confused. When they drove to the middle of Salt Lake City, he was even more confused. Now, watching them swallowed up by this innocuous looking suburb, he was downright perplexed.

Where on earth are they going? he wondered. He reached under his seat and retrieved a handgun in a battered leather holster. "There's only one way to find out."

21

Ammon Rogers now knew what Alice had felt like when she had fallen down the rabbit hole. Standing where someone's back yard, patio furniture, and lawn toys should have existed, some of the most peculiar and eclectic works of art Ammon had ever seen confronted him. The scale of some of the works added to the surreal nature of the scene: several of the pieces towered over the site.

A stone man, holding a sword, was carved into a fifteen-foot tall stone slab, an irregularly shaped boulder where the head should have been. To the east of the armed giant sat a large brick furnace near what appeared to be a stone altar. Further east stood an arch made of large white stones built between a tall spire hewn from solid rock and a stack of four stone books. Toward the middle of the property loomed an artificial hill constructed of boulders. Inside a large recess in this hill were two stone hands reaching down toward a pair of stone hearts.

In the approximate center of it all stood the object they had come to see. The Joseph Smith Sphinx was not a completely carved monument like its Egyptian counterpart, but a pile of large stones shaped to resemble the famous landmark, its highest point approximately ten feet high. The only finished portion of the work was the head and chest. The head was carved with the likeness of the Prophet, clad in his familiar upturned collar and cravat. Other than these recognizable features, this was by no means a standard portrait. The artist had arrayed Joseph in the triangular headpiece of the Sphinx, and an odd carving took the place of the shirtfront. Ammon initially took it for a castle wall covered with stars. Surrounding these and other sculptures were well-manicured lawns and beautiful beds of flowers.

"Who would make such a place?" Ammon said aloud.

"His name was Thomas B. Child," Sariah replied at his back.

"Don't tell me you learned that in Primary?" Ammon asked, turning toward his wife.

"No, silly, it says so in this pamphlet," she responded holding up a small booklet.

"Where did you get that?"

"Over there," Sariah pointed toward the entrance. "There was a rack full of them."

"Oh."

"Anyway…says in here that Thomas Child was a successful masonry contractor, community leader and served nineteen years as a bishop. He started building these sculptures in his late fifties as an expression of his faith," said Sariah.

"Man, I know I grew up less active, but what does this stuff have to do with the church?"

"Well, as odd as some of his art might appear, there is a certain logic to it all. Take our friend the Sphinx here; the booklet says, '*The Sphinx represents Child's belief that the answers to life's great questions cannot be discovered with the intellect, but only through faith. The sphinx is an ancient symbol of riddles and mystery. Joseph Smith's face symbolizes Child's conviction that the LDS Priesthood reveals to mankind the answers to life's mysteries.*' "[21]

"I guess so," Ammon reluctantly admitted.

"Look, here's our poem," Sariah said, pointing to the ground near the left paw of the sphinx.

"Sure enough," Ammon confirmed, coming to his wife's side, "but how does that help us find our numbers?"

"The poem? I told you, I don't think anything. There are no lines going from it to any of the blank spaces of the coordinated," Sariah replied. "What it does do is get us in the right vicinity. Look at these two riddles." She removed the folded sheet of paper from her jacket. Ammon placed his chin on her shoulder and gazed at the document over her shoulder.

"The two riddles in the bottom left corner both have the word *seer* in them," Sariah continued. "This one says, *Behind the seer lies a field of white,* and this one, *Remove six of the seer's stars from the portal directly in front.*"

"But what does any of that mean? It's a bunch of gibberish." Ammon said, with obvious frustration.

"Taking for granted that the sphinx is the seer, then it must be something here in the vicinity."

"But what?" Ammon replied.

"Let's look at them one at a time," Sariah returned. This lower one… *Remove six of the seer's stars from the portal directly in front.*"

"There are some stars carved on the chest of the sphinx," Ammon replied.

"I saw that," Sariah said, walking around to the front of the impressive work.

"It looks like the big dipper on the wall of a castle or something," said Ammon.

"It's not a castle; it looks familiar, though…" Sariah tapped her lips, thinking. "Of course!" She jumped up. "It's the Salt Lake Temple!"

"The Salt Lake temple has the Big Dipper carved on it?" asked Ammon.

"Yeah," Sariah said. "That is a representation of it on the sphinx's chest."

"That's all well and good," Ammon said, looking around, "but I don't see any portals in front of him. There are some houses over there, but—"

Sariah cut in. "My guess is that we will have to go to Temple Square and take a look around. I think this is a riddle within a riddle."

"You're probably right," Ammon agreed. "It couldn't be easy could it? Oh, well. What does the other one say again?"

"*Behind the seer lies a field of white,*" read Sariah.

"Great!" Ammon exclaimed. "Is that another riddle within a riddle, because I don't see any fields around here, let alone a pasty one?"

"No silly," Sariah said. "In the scriptures, when it says a field is white, it doesn't mean that the plants are actually white, but that it is ready to be harvested."

"Okay, so…I don't see anything like that either," Ammon replied.

"What do you see, then?"

"I see more weird statues and engravings in rock."

"Well, let's look around. Maybe something will jump out at us," Sariah said, resignedly.

The young couple began examining the works of art behind the sphinx. Sariah walked to the north side of the artificial hill and Ammon stayed on the south. After a short time, Ammon called to his wife, "Hey Sariah!"

"Yes?"

"You said 'white field' is a term from the scriptures?"

"Yeah, so?" Sariah responded, walking around the hill.

"There's a bunch of them carved in these rocks here," Ammon said pointing to the base of the artificial hill.

"That's better than what I found," Sariah responded.

"What?"

"A bunch of stone body parts."

"Really?"

"Yeah, a representation of King Nebuchadnezzar's dream," Sariah said.

"King Nebucha… who?"

"Never mind. What scriptures are they?"

"These here are from the Doctrine and Covenants. Any of these refer to white fields?" Ammon asked.

"Not sure," Sariah replied shaking her head. "I don't have *all* of the standard works memorized, ya know."

Ammon opened his mouth in mock amazement and then asked, "So now what?"

"Call Kevin," Sariah stated, flatly.

"Oh…all right."

Sariah retrieved her phone from her pocket and hit speed dial.

Ammon looked at his watch. "Five after seven. You think he's up?"

Sariah shrugged her shoulders. After only two rings a surprisingly awake sounding Kevin answered, "Good morning sunshine! Wait, are we on speaker phone?"

"Yes," Ammon responded.

"Oh…Good morning to you too, Ammon," Kevin retorted.

"Did I wake you up?" Sariah asked.

"Nope," Kevin replied proudly. "Haven't been to sleep yet!"

Ammon rolled his eyes.

"Okay," Sariah responded. "Then I guess you won't mind looking something up for us?"

"Sure…Oh, wait! Guess last night's raid was too much for my computer. I've gotta re-boot. Let me call you back in a minute."

"Alright," Sariah replied, and hung up.

As they waited, Ammon's eyes wandered to the small cave he had noticed earlier. Although the stone hearts and hands still bewildered him, seeing the cave reminded him of something he had meant to ask.

"Sariah?"

"Yes?"

"Remember yesterday when your dad mentioned his lecture on the Seven Caves legend and its relationship to the Book of Mormon, or something like that?"

"I guess so."

"Tell me about it. It sounds interesting."

"It is very interesting," Sariah answered her husband. "And it certainly does relate to this little adventure of ours. You see, both the Aztecs and the Mayans refer to seven sacred caves in their creation stories. They are not identical, but both say something along the lines of how their ancestors were one of seven groups that came out of sacred caves."[22]

"Okay," Ammon said, nodding, "but, what does that have to do with The Book of Mormon?"

"Well, The Book of Mormon normally divides, in a literary sense, the people up into two camps, Lamanites and Nephites, right?"

"Yes," replied Ammon.

"The book, however, also states that this is done for the sake of simplicity and that there was actually more diversity among the people."

"Really?"

"Yes," Sariah replied. "It says in three different places, that the people considered themselves either a Nephite, Jacobite, Josephite, Zoramite, Lamanite, Lemuelite or an Ishmaelite.[23] There are multiple references to this, spread out along the entire timeline of The Book of Mormon, showing this was an enduring concept."

"Those were the seven original groups?" Ammon replied.

"Yup," Sariah returned. "The seven founding tribes, you could say. Just like the Aztecs and Mayans believed."

"A coincidence?"

"Sure," Sariah responded, skeptically.

"What does all of that have to do with Carre-Shinob?" Ammon asked.

"So, our friends the Aztecs believed the sacred cave they came out of was none other than Carre-Shinob. They also believed much of their gold came from there in the first place. It makes perfect sense that when calamity struck, they wanted to take their treasure and sacred relics to Carre-Shinob. They wanted to take it all home."

The phone rang, startling both of them. Sariah blew out a long breath, smiled at Ammon and answered. It was Kevin.

"Okay…Sorry about that. What do you need me to look up?"

"Go to LDS.org and then to the D&C page."

"Okay, got it," Kevin said, after a short pause.

"Can you tell us if any of the following sections have the phrase *the field is white* in them," Sariah asked.

"Let me grab a pencil…Okay, shoot."

"One, four, fifty, seventy-six, eighty-four, eighty-eight, or ninety-three."

"Hold on…How 'bout D&C 4:4 *For behold the field is white already to harvest; and lo, he that thrusteth in his sickle with his might, the same layeth up in store that he perisheth not, but bringeth salvation to his soul;*"

Ammon and Sariah looked at each other with wide smiles on their faces. "I think we got our first number!" Ammon exclaimed.

"Thanks Kevin! We'll probably be calling again," Sariah said.

"I look forward to it!"

Sariah put her phone away and wrote the number four in the appropriate blank. "One down. I wonder how my dad is doing."

"Speaking of your dad, there's one thing you still have never told me," Ammon said.

"Oh yeah?" Sariah asked suspiciously.

"Yeah, are you ever going to tell me where John is from?"

"I've tried about fifty times before, but we always seem to get interrupted," Sariah replied, defensively. "If you must know, he was born in..."

A sudden strong sensation arrested Ammon's attention. It was the tingling sensation at the back of his neck that had saved his life many times. Reflexively, he said to his wife, "Quick, don't ask questions; hide the riddles!"

Sariah knew to trust her husband's premonitions. She promptly slipped the map inside her jacket, as Ammon heard an all-too-familiar click. Turning slowly around he saw that, for the second time in as many days, he had a gun pointed at him. This time, however, the man holding the weapon looked intent on using it.

22
1521 A.D.

As Tlahuicle looked at the men now gathered around him, his heart swelled with pride and gratitude. True to their word, all of the royal porters who had wintered with the different Nuche tribes returned when summoned. They were ready to complete their sacred mission.

The completion of their duty was not, however, without sadness. Many of the men were busy consoling their grieving Nuche wives. Some even gently patted the bellies of those women who were with child. Tlahuicle envied them. These men, and eventually the others, would have offspring to remember them when they were gone, their brave deeds recited around the winter fire for generations to come. Tlahuicle would not be so fortunate. There would be no little one to remember his name once he left this world.

At least, he thought gazing at fifty very special bundles sitting on the ground, *the voice of my people will not be lost.*

The fifty packages were the most important of all the other hundreds upon hundreds of burdens about to make their way into the mountains. Protecting these particular items from Cortez was one of the main reasons Montezuma had ordered them into the wilderness. In keeping them safe, they protected the memory of the Aztec people and their ancestors.

It is time to begin, Tlahuicle thought. He bowed to the Chief of the Tumpanawachs as a sign of gratitude, called his men to their burdens, and turned his face toward the melting snows high above him.

23

Present Day

"Let me see your hands," Travis Stanwick ordered, his gun leveled exactly at Ammon's chest.

"What do you want?" Ammon demanded.

"I'll tell you what I want, son," Travis snapped. "I want what your little missy stashed away in her jacket there."

Ammon and Sariah looked at each other out of the corners of their eyes.

Who is this guy? Ammon thought. Turning his eyes on the stranger, he wondered if the man had raided John Wayne's wardrobe. Clad in snakeskin boots, blue jeans, brown duster coat, and a black Stetson cowboy hat, the gunman looked like he belonged on the open range and not in downtown Salt Lake City.

"I don't know what you're talking about," Sariah said.

"Now, now missy," Travis returned. "I saw the whole thing. Hand me the map and no one gets hurt."

Before Ammon could think of what to do next Sariah said defiantly, "Fine! You want it you can have it!"

She then reached into her jacket, grabbed a piece of paper and threw it into the air. Watching in horror, Ammon saw the paper catch in the morning breeze and blow completely across the sculpture park. Travis screamed and raced off after the flying pamphlet.

Ammon turned to join him when Sariah caught hold of his arm and said, "Come on! Let's get out of here!"

"But—the riddles!" Ammon said, frantically.

"Don't worry," Sariah said calmly. "I threw the Gilgal Gardens brochure I picked up earlier. Hurry, it won't take him long to figure it out!"

"I could kiss you right now," Ammon's face flooded with relief.

"Later. Let's go," Sariah smiled.

They tore off together toward the retaining wall and fence at the north of the gardens and made it over without too much difficulty. To their great surprise, they were now standing in the middle of a Chuck-O-Rama parking lot. From normal looking houses to a bizarre landscape of stone, to a Chuck-O-Rama all in less than fifty yards. *This certainly is not your normal neighborhood*, Ammon thought.

In the middle of the parking lot was a large tour bus disembarking Japanese tourists.

"What are they doing here?" Sariah asked. "They're too early for lunch."

"I don't know, but it gives me an idea," Ammon replied. He took Sariah by the hand and walked calmly toward the tourists who had gathered in a large group near the side of their bus. The Japanese smiled and bowed at the young couple. Ammon returned these gestures by pointing between the tourists and their bus and then putting his right index finger in front of his mouth in what he hoped was the universal symbol for quiet.

Whatever it really meant to the Japanese, it achieved the desired effect. The group parted, allowed Ammon and Sariah to enter, and then closed ranks. The two crouched down, effectively hiding them between the milling group and the bus.

"I hope you know what you're doing," Sariah said, softly.

"Me too."

The proof of this concept was going to come sooner rather than later. A shout of dismay and the scuffling of cowboy boots on asphalt told Ammon and Sariah their mysterious new friend had entered the parking lot. Ammon held his breath and Sariah grabbed his hand and held it tightly. Any second, they expected to hear their assailant's harsh condescending voice. Instead, they heard something unexpected.

"Oooohhhh…Cowboy!" One of the tourists said, spotting Travis walking toward them.

"Cowboy! Cowboy!" The other Japanese took up the call excitedly.

Peeking up through the crowd Ammon saw the tour group crowding around the gunman, patting him on the back, taking pictures of him, even trying to take pictures *with* him. This was obviously the first American they had ever seen clad in western wear, and they acted as if the man had walked right off the movie screen. His eyes darted back and forth like a cornered animal. He tried to wiggle free from the group, but the throng was too great. He was, for all intents and purposes, trapped.

Seizing their chance, Ammon and Sariah crawled under the bus on their stomachs and ran toward the front of the restaurant.

"I don't know how long our friends will keep that guy busy, but we have to get to the car," Ammon said.

Ammon and Sariah circled the block to the east and reached their car in no time at all. They quickly climbed in and Ammon fired up the middle-aged Toyota sedan.

"Uh oh!" Sariah exclaimed, as they were backing out. "We've got company again!"

Ammon whipped his head around just in time to see their assailant run out of the iron gate marking the entrance to Gilgal.

"Who is this homicidal cowboy, anyway?" Ammon popped the car into drive and hit the gas. "With all of the people trying to kill me lately, I'm starting to get a complex."

"It's not you; it's the gold," Sariah answered, solemnly. "Death and violence have followed it for hundreds of years."

Behind them, the man cried out in frustration.

"You're not getting away that easy!" he yelled, jumping into his truck. The aged starter motor finally brought the choking engine to life. He was back on Ammon and Sariah's tail, although this time they knew it. They made a quick right and then a left onto Fourth South, heading west. Within a block, the old truck was right behind Ammon and Sariah.

"What do we do?" Sariah asked, her voice full of concern.

"I don't know," Ammon responded. "Maybe we could look for a police station. I think we will be fine until then. I don't think he would try anything out here in the—"

A sudden powerful lurch and the crunch of metal cut him short.

He's ramming us! This lunatic is ramming us! This guy must be really desperate. Ammon thought. A check in his rearview mirror confirmed this assessment; he saw the flinty stare and set jaw of their shadow. He had no doubt this man would stop at nothing to get his hands on the paper tucked safely away in Sariah's jacket.

"I'm already sick of this. Hold on!" Ammon said, as they neared Fourth East. He maneuvered the car into the far right lane and flicked his right turn signal on. An eastbound Trax train neared the intersection as well. The pursuing truck fell in behind them.

"What are you going to do?" Sariah shouted.

"Just hold on!"

Ammon slowed down as if to turn right, then, at the last second, cranked the wheel hard to the left and jammed his foot on the gas pedal. The Toyota cut across the inner two lanes of traffic, flew into the intersection and then rocketed southbound on Fourth East, barely missing the lead Trax car. A chorus of angry honks and one ominous train horn chastised Ammon for his risky maneuver.

"Good," Ammon said triumphantly after making a series of random right and left turns and then checking the rear view mirror. "I think we lost him."

"What just happened?" Sariah asked. She sounded very calm, almost to the point of being detached from the situation.

"Oh that?" Ammon responded, with a short laugh. "That was a little move I picked up in Army tactical driving school. If someone is following you, make it seem like you're going to turn right, then quickly turn left across traffic. It's a good way to shake a pursuer."

"And the train?" Sariah asked, in the same far off tone.

"That? Just luck. No way he was going to follow us through that, eh?"

"I see," Sariah said, sedately. Suddenly, she turned in her seat and punched her husband hard in the shoulder.

"Oww!" Ammon cried out.

"That's for not warning me!"

She then leaned over and kissed him on the cheek, tenderly, "And that is for being amazing."

"Thanks…I guess."

"Okay. Turn here," Sariah continued. "This will get us to Temple Square. Those riddles aren't going to solve themselves."

24

Gazing around Temple Square, Ammon Rogers was surprised at how crowded it was this early in the morning. The beautiful grounds were flooded with tourists, families, and individuals, all eager to see the magnificent temple and accompanying attractions. Groups of sister missionaries were busy conversing with people and answering questions.

Passing one such group, Ammon heard an Asian sister recounting the story of Joseph Smith's First Vision. Another sister further down the concourse directed a tourist to the famous Christus statue in a British accent. He thought they might need to ask for directions to a Big Dipper carved on the Temple, but he was mistaken. Sariah marched directly to the west side of the building and looked up. He joined her. There, high above the flagpole, were the seven stars of the Big Dipper carved in relief on the middle spire directly above the highest window. The handle stars pointed down, the cup open to the north.

"Well," Sariah said. "There it is."

"Sure enough," Ammon replied.

"I can't believe you didn't notice it the *last* time we were here," Sariah commented.

"Why?" Ammon took her hand, kissing it. "Who has time for obscure masonry when there's a beautiful bride to gawk at?"

"Correct answer," Sariah returned, patting his cheek.

"Can I ask a stupid question, though?"

"Why does the temple have the Big Dipper carved on it?" Sariah responded.

"Yeah."

"It's symbolic," said Sariah. "Something along the line of: 'As the Big Dipper helps the lost traveler find his way by locating the North Star, the Temple helps lost souls find their way back to God.' "[24]

"That makes sense," Ammon said, nodding. "What doesn't make sense is this riddle. What does it say, again?"

Sariah retrieved the paper from her jacket. "*Remove six of the seer's stars from the portal directly in front,*" she read.

"If these are the seer's stars, I don't see anything directly in front, other than the Tabernacle," Ammon said, turning toward the large, met-al-roofed building. In so doing, he saw Sariah leaving his side, walking toward one of the many entrances of the grand structure. Catching up with her, Ammon found her scrutinizing a small plaque above the door.

"What does that say?" she asked.

"It's the number thirteen,' He responded.

"What is another name for a door?"

"Oh, I don't know. *Entrance?*"

"How about *portal?*" Sariah said.

"Yeah, okay—Wait!" Ammon whirled around, his heart thumping in his chest. The stars of the Big Dipper were directly behind him.

"Take the six stars away from the number thirteen above the door and you get…" Sariah started.

"Seven!" Ammon finished.

Sariah carefully wrote the newly discovered number into the appropriate blank, joining their discovery from Gilgal Gardens. Ammon saw her hand was shaking slightly with what he guessed was excitement.

12 T 0 5 _ 6 5 _ _. _ _ ME
4 5 1 7 1 _ _. _ _ MN

"Now we're getting somewhere!" Ammon said, triumphantly. "Now what?"

"Well, this riddle says, *Number two read this chapter to two,*" Sariah read.

"Number two what?"

"We've seen the Joseph Smith Sphinx…maybe number two refers to Brigham Young," Sariah said, thoughtfully.

"Is there anything in this town directly related to him?" Ammon asked.

"How about everything," Sariah snorted. "His house, his grave, a museum filled with his processions; his stamp is all over this town."

"I see your point," Ammon sighed.

"Unfortunately, I can't think of anything that has to do with reading," Sariah said, twisting her mouth.

"So, his house is still standing?"

"He actually had several homes," Sariah nodded her head. "The main one is about a block east from here. Why?"

"Oh, I was just thinking: maybe the riddle has something to do with his old library or office or something," said Ammon, shrugging his shoulders.

"Possibly," Sariah shrugged her shoulders, too. "It's as good a place to start as any—uh-oh!"

Noting the concern in his wife's voice, Ammon followed her gaze. To the south of where they stood a black cowboy hat bobbed among the masses like a cork adrift on a pond. As the man neared, Ammon saw the determined face of their friend from the sculpture garden. He walked slowly along the walk and made no sign that he saw Ammon and Sariah standing by the Tabernacle.

"He's here," Ammon said in a low voice. "How'd he find us?"

"I don't know," Sariah replied. "We hid our car pretty well in the back of the parking terrace."

"He might not even know we're here," Ammon returned. "We'd better get a move on!"

Turning to leave, Ammon ran into something that felt like a brick wall.

"Hi, coach," the wall greeted him warmly.

"Sione!" Ammon responded. "Hi." Ammon had not in fact run into a wall, but rather one of the football players he helped train as a part-time job. Sione was a mountain of a man, standing six-feet-six-inches tall and weighing well over three hundred pounds. He had graduated from college and worked out at the training facility, staying sharp for the NFL draft. Although he usually only worked with high school players, Ammon had come to know Sione pretty well due to his interest in Ammon's war stories. To Ammon's amazement, two men just as large—if not larger—than Sione flanked him.

"What are you doing here?" Ammon asked, momentarily forgetting his plight.

"My brothers and I came to see our cousin. She just started her mission here," Sione responded.

"Oh, cool," Ammon said. A tug on his arm from Sariah reminded him that he had other concerns besides this man's relatives.

Ammon was about to take his leave of Sione when a fiendishly delightful idea popped into his head.

"Hey Sione, see that guy coming this way, wearing a black cowboy hat?" Ammon asked.

"Yeah. What about him?"

"He's, uh, giving my wife and me some trouble. Could you, uh…ask him to leave us alone?" Ammon asked, trying to keep a straight face.

The broad, friendly, smile on Sione's face melted into an impish grin.

"Sure, coach; we'll teach him some respect for women."

"Thanks, man! See you next week," Ammon said.

Sione did not respond. He and his two companions were already heading straight for the unsuspecting man. Somewhere deep down, Ammon felt pity for him. The sensation did not last long.

Sariah grabbed Ammon by the hand and they ran toward the opposite gate.

"Is it a sin to have someone beat up on Temple Square?" Sariah asked, reaching the outside sidewalk.

"How should I know?" Ammon retuned, with a wink. "I never went to Primary, remember?"

25

Orson Campbell drained the final contents of the white porcelain mug, got up from the counter, paid his bill and strode out of the café adjacent to the Frontier Motel. He felt flush with excitement. The happenings of the last ten hours were incredible. It had started out like any other evening: sitting in the Frontier Grill, talking to other prospectors. The subtle verbal ballet in these conversations always amused Orson. The goal was to coax new information from your competitors without divulging too much yourself. To get something, you generally had to give something up; the trick was not giving too much. The intricacies of these negotiations could be the envy of any boardroom in cooperate America.

The hope was always to find someone new to town: someone not familiar with the game, someone with new clues regarding the whereabouts of some gold. Yesterday evening had started out like the hundred before it.

For the most part, the same old faces stared at him from the same old tables and counter. A few tourists ate and departed, but he knew they lacked anything of use to him. He recognized the look in a man's eye when gold fever was running high. None of these folks wanted after the same thing he did.

After eating and sitting around for two hours, Orson was ready to concede another wasted night. He was about to rise from his seat when something froze him to his chair. Into the Frontier walked a rather unlikely pair: a young Ute, looking both sad and nervous, accompanied by a middle-aged man in khakis. Orson could not put his finger on it, but the man in the khakis looked familiar. The older of the two scanned the inside of the café as if looking for someone. Unsuccessful, he sought out one of the waitresses. Orson could not hear what anyone said, but the men nodded disappointedly and left.

"What those fellers want?" Orson inquired of the waitress.

"Oh, they was looking for Old Mike," she responded, setting down her tray at a booth.

"Old Mike the Ute?"

"None other." She began picking up the dishes and litter left on the table.

"What'd they want him for?" Orson asked, his curiosity piqued. The local treasure hunters suspected that Old Mike knew the location of lost gold mines in the area, but he never told them anything, no matter how much they begged, bartered, or—some of them—threatened. Some people followed him from time to time when he walked in the mountains, but to no avail. Two strangers looking for Old Mike might mean something.

"They didn't say," the waitress responded.

"Well, what'd ya tell 'em?"

"I told 'em he usually comes in mornin's, and they should try back tomorrow."

"What'd they say?" He smiled amiably at the server.

"Oh, they was disappointed, but they thanked me kindly and said they'd be back in the mornin'."

This was all that Orson needed to hear. He left the Frontier that night feeling more hopeful than he had in a long time. Not wanting to miss these new comers or Old Mike, Orson arrived at the café early the next morning. At eight-thirty, Old Mike made his way inside, looking like he had been up all night. Not long after, the two strangers walked in. It was then, after a night's reflection, that Orson recognized the older man: John Byrd. Byrd was infamous among treasure hunters for the hypocrisy of warning other hunters away from Spanish gold, while he himself was reputed to own a sizeable amount. John Byrd seeking out Old Mike: this must be good.

John and his young companion quickly located Old Mike and sat down opposite him at his table. From his position, Orson was once again unable to hear what they said, but he had a clear view. He watched carefully as Old Mike listened intently to John and then resolutely shook his head. The young Ute pled with Old Mike. Orson saw the young man wipe his eyes as he spoke. As impassioned as this plea was, it also met a negative response from the old Ute. He refused a last entreaty from John, and they rose and departed.

Standing on the street, squinting in the morning sun, Orson scratched his head, perplexed by this turn of events. Maybe it was nothing; then again… Orson thought for a moment and then made up his mind.

"Better get the boys together," he said aloud, walking purposefully toward his pickup.

26

" Sariah, come here," Ammon called to his wife. "Check this out."

Sariah left the sister missionaries to conduct their tour of the Beehive House and joined her husband. They stood on the first floor in a room directly behind Brigham Young's office.

"What is it?" she asked.

Ammon stood by a row of framed photographs of Brigham Young, hanging on a wall and arranged by age, starting with the youngest version of the prophet on the far left side. Ammon pointed to a photograph, a very young-looking Brigham standing in a doorway. On his head stood the tallest stovepipe hat Ammon had ever seen, a hat that would make Abraham Lincoln green with envy.

"Yeah, so?" said Sariah.

"When Chief Walker said he saw the High Hats, he wasn't kidding." Ammon laughed.

"Laugh if you want," Sariah grinned, "but this picture illustrates how spot-on his vision was, doesn't it?"

Their guides smiled politely and continued the tour.

"And this is President Young's study," Sister Romney, the tour guide, said with a sweep of her arm.

His study! Ammon thought. *This might have something to do with reading.* A table, adorned with two large books, occupied the center of the room. A combination writing desk and hutch stood in the corner. Rows of books waited behind glass doors. Two armchairs pointed toward the fireplace, perfectly arranged for a comfortable reading session on a cold winter's night.

Looking around the room, however, Ammon saw nothing that appeared to have any connection to the riddle. Not even the three paintings on the wall fit the riddle. One was a stylized portrait of the Young family, showing several children. One was a profile of Joseph Smith, and the last was a battle scene of some sort. Sariah must have reached the same conclusion.

"Excuse me?" she asked the tour guides. "I know this is an off-the-wall question, but is there anything in this room or the rest of the house that has anything to do with President Young reading? Possibly to two people? I don't know, maybe to his kids or something."

"Nothing specific comes to mind," Sister Romney responded, after a moment's reflection. "There is a large book case on the second floor, as well as the school room. That room, along with the rest of this house, would have been full of children. I can't imagine him reading a story to only two children."

"Are there any pictures or depictions of him reading?" Ammon asked.

"Not that I know of. It wouldn't surprise me, though. President Young *was* a great proponent of education and learning. In fact, he is credited for establishing two universities in Utah."

"I imagine one of them is BYU," Ammon replied. "What's the other one?"

"Ironically enough, the University of Utah," Sister Romney said, proudly.

"Wow, did you know that?" Ammon asked, turning toward Sariah.

"Uh, yeah," Sariah responded, obviously annoyed at the insult to her intelligence.

"That is ironic," Ammon continued. "BYU and the U of U, founded by the same person. It's a wonder they hate each other so much."

At the conclusion of the tour, Ammon and Sariah found themselves standing back on the sidewalk in front of the Beehive House.

"Well, now what?" Ammon asked, dejectedly.

"I don't know," Sariah replied. "Maybe we could—"

"Excuse me," a female voice interrupted.

Ammon and Sariah looked up and saw their tour guide, Sister Romney, hurrying down the front steps.

"Yes?" Sariah responded.

"I'm so glad I caught you."

"Oh. Why?" Ammon asked

"Yes. Um, I was intrigued by your question, so I related it to another one of the sisters and she reminded me of something that might interest you."

Ammon and Sariah shot each other a quick excited glance and then simultaneously asked, "What is it?"

"Not too far from here is a statue of Brigham Young," she replied.

"So?" Ammon responded.

Sister Romney raised her eyebrows and then said, "It depicts him reading to two children."

27

Turning their car east onto First Avenue, Ammon glanced over at the gleaming Angel Moroni atop the temple. It looked magnificent, especially knowing what he knew now.

"So Moroni's golden skin really came from Carre-Shinob, eh?" he asked.

"It only stands to reason," Sariah responded.

"You know, I've seen him dozens of times over the years and never thought a thing about it. And now, I know this sounds weird, but he doesn't…"

"Seem like a statue anymore? It's kind of like a real person, isn't it?" Sariah finished.

"Yeah!"

"I feel the same way," Sariah answered. "I think it comes from knowing the whole story."

"Maybe."

"We're here; find a spot and pull over," said Sariah.

"We're where?" Ammon asked, looking around.

"The cemetery where Brigham Young is buried," Sariah responded.

"Where?"

"Right there."

Ammon parked and they exited the vehicle. All Ammon could see is what appeared to be a small park tucked between two buildings.

"This is a cemetery?" Ammon asked.

"A small private one, yes. They buried President Young here, along with some of his family. I knew about this place, but I've never been here before. "

Walking down a flight of stone stairs, a small tidy multi-tiered park came into full view.

"That must be his grave down there in the corner," Sariah said, pointing to a granite slab surrounded by a waist-high metal fence. In the lower courtyard, there were other non-fenced stone slab grave markers. A stone pedestal bearing a small metal bust of the second president of the Church stood in the center of the yard.

"And that's what we came to see," Sariah said, pointing west of center. There under a small clump of trees stood, or rather sat, a bronze statue of Brigham Young. The work represented the prophet resting on a metal bench, reading a book to a small girl seated on his lap, while an older boy stood behind him and peered over his shoulder. Next to Brigham on the bench sat another open metal book.

"Number two reading to two?" Ammon said.

"I'd say so!" Sariah responded, hurrying toward the small metallic group, "but what chapter?"

Ammon walked around to the back of the statue and squinted at the book in the Prophet's hand.

"It says the Book of Nephi…chapter V," he reported to his wife.

"That's a Roman numeral. It means chapter five," she replied.

"There we go!" Ammon said, exultantly. "We got another one."

"I'm not so sure," Sariah added, tapping her finger on her pursed lips.

"Why not?" Ammon asked. "It fits the riddle: number two reads to two."

"The riddle says that number two *read* this chapter to two," countered Sariah. "This is a depiction of number two *reading* to two."

"What's the answer, then?" Ammon asked.

"Maybe it's the book next to him," Sariah returned. "He *read* that book to the two children, set it aside, and is now *reading* the Book of Mormon to them."

Leaning over the book Ammon said, "John X?"

"That's the New Testament, John, chapter ten. That's got to be it," Sariah responded, already writing on the paper.

While Sariah busied herself with the paper, Ammon walked toward Brigham's grave.

"This is it?" Ammon said in amazement.

"Is what it?" Sariah returned.

"This…" Ammon said, waving his hand toward the grave. "I mean, this guy rallied the Church after Joseph Smith was killed, oversaw one of the largest human migrations in American history, and colonized a large chunk of the west, and there is no spacious tomb or large stone monuments?"

"It's fitting, really," Sariah replied.

"How so?"

"Well, Brigham Young was, and is, a hero to some and a villain to others, but when it is all said and done, he was simply a humble servant of the Lord."

"Good point," conceded Ammon.

He returned to the seated prophet and then asked, "Are you sure 'ten' is the answer?"

"Pretty sure," Sariah responded. The number ten takes care of two blanks. This would explain why the line from the riddle points between two blanks rather than directly at one. The number five would only fill one spot."

"Can't argue with that," said Ammon. "Now, what?"

"Well, this one here on the side has two lines pointing toward double blanks on separate lines. If we get that one, we're over half-way done," Sariah responded.

"Tell me what it says again."

"*Under chapter and verse sleeps Cornelius's bane,*" Sariah read.

"What's a Cornelius?" Ammon asked.

"It's the name of a guy. It seems like I should know the significance, but I can't put my finger on it."

"The *sleeping under* part has to be referring to a grave, right?" asked Ammon.

"I'm sure it does," Sariah replied, "but without knowing who Cornelius is, we can't possibly know who his bane was or where they are buried."

"I know what that means," Ammon said, his voice full of dread.

Sariah removed her phone from her pocket and dialed the number.

"Hello, beautiful!" Kevin Mitchell answer. "How's your little scavenger hunt going?"

"Fine," Sariah responded, "but we've hit another dead end. Do you think you could look something up for us again?"

"Shoot."

"Okay. Search for the name Cornelius in conjunction with church history."

After a short pause, Kevin said, "Okay, a guy named Cornelius P. Lott keeps popping up."

"Oh, that name is so familiar," Sariah agonized. "What is he known for?"

"Let's see…ooh! Ol' Cornelius has his own Wikipedia page! Let's look there."

At Kevin's response, Ammon's eye twitched.

"Okay, let's see," Kevin began. "Born blah blah blah, married, blah blah blah, and… Now, this is interesting. It seems our friend Cornelius is best known for trying to dissuade Mary Fielding Smith from immigrating to Utah and then antagonizing her along the way when she went anyway."

"That's it!" Sariah cried. "I knew that name sounded familiar. Cornelius's bane is Mary Fielding Smith!"

"Who is Mary Fielding Smith?" Ammon inquired.

"I'll tell you in a minute," Sariah said, raised a finger signaling Ammon to hold on. "Say Kevin, could you tell us where Mary is buried?"

"Sure," Kevin replied, proudly. "She is buried in the Salt Lake City cemetery."

"Wonderful!" exclaimed Sariah. "Can you tell us where exactly in the cemetery the grave is located? We need to see her tombstone."

"Sure, I guess, but I have a picture of it right here on her Wikipedia pages," Kevin returned.

"You do?" Sariah said. "What does it say?"

"It says…*Sacred to the memory of Mary relict of Patriarch Hyrum Smith who died Sept. 21, 1852 in the 52nd year of her age. She died as she had lived near 17 years, firm in the faith of the Gospel. Blessed are the dead which die in the Lord. Rev.14c.13v.*"

"Rev fourteen see thirteen vee," Ammon repeated.

"It's got to be Revelation, chapter fourteen, verse thirteen," replied Sariah. "Thanks Kevin."

"Talk to you soon?" Kevin asked, with pleasure.

"I'm sure," Sariah said, and then terminated the call.

"Are you sure those are the right numbers?" Ammon asked. "I mean, whoever she was, it sounds like Cornelius was her bane, not vice versa."

"Oh no," Sariah countered. "Mary Fielding Smith was definitely Cornelius P. Lott's bane."

"Who is she? A relative of Joseph Smith's?" Ammon asked, and then quickly added, "And no, I never went to Primary, I was out running an illegal dog racing track, remember?"

"Ha ha," Sariah responded, sarcastically. "Mary Fielding Smith was the sister-in-law of Joseph Smith. She was married to his brother, Hyrum."

"Why is she the bane of poor old Cornelius?"

"Well, after her husband and brother-in-law were martyred, she desperately wanted to emigrate to Utah along with the other saints. Cornelius P. Lott was a captain of one of the wagon trains and tried to talk her out of going."

"Why?"

"He said she wasn't prepared for the journey and claimed that she would slow the whole group down," Sariah responded.

"What'd she do?"

"She told him unequivocally, that she was going and that nothing would stop her. She even told him she would beat him to the Salt Lake valley."

"Did she?" Ammon asked.

"Oh, yes," Sariah responded, "but not without the help of several miracles."[25]

"Miracles?"

"Yup."

"What kind of miracles?" Ammon asked.

"Well, one day they were traveling along and Mary's best ox collapsed."

"Collapsed?" Ammon echoed. "That's rough."

"Yes, collapsed and appeared to be dead. To make matters worse, Cornelius rode by at that very moment, gave her a big fat *I told you so*, and rode on."

"What did she do?"

"Without missing a beat, she had her brother and a friend give the beast a blessing," Sariah said.

"A blessing?"

"Yeah," Sariah answered. "To heal him."

"Huh. I did not know you could administer to an animal. Did it work?"

"It sure did! The ox stood up immediately and started pulling the wagon, as if nothing had ever happened."

"Cool," Ammon said, duly impressed. "What other miraculous things happened?"

"There were other animal healing episodes," Sariah said, "but the most peculiar thing happened when they were literally in sight of the Salt Lake valley."

"Oh yeah, what was that?"

"As you can imagine, our friend Cornelius was irked that *his* prophecies of Mary's failure had not come to pass. He definitely did not want *her* prophecy about beating him to the valley to come true. When the wagon company woke up one morning and saw Mary's cattle had wandered off, he was not too broken up about it."

"What did he do?" Ammon asked.

"Nothing to help her, that's for sure," Sariah said. "He gave the order for the rest of the company to move on and leave her behind."

"How did she beat him into the valley, then?"

"That's the miraculous part," Sariah added, raising her eyebrows. "Even though it had been a crystal clear fall morning, a freak storm appeared out of nowhere. The ensuing thunder and lightning spooked the hitched teams of the company, making them unmanageable."

"What did they do?"

"All of the animals had to be unhitched and they subsequently ran off in a panic. Somehow, however, during all of this, Mary's group had managed to collect all of their oxen, hitch 'em up, and ride off toward Salt Lake."

"While the others were chasing their strays," Ammon added.

"Yup," Sariah said. "Mary beat the rest of the company into the Salt Lake Valley by a day. I guess you could say the Lord helped Mary win her bet."

"Hmm," Ammon said. "That is a strange story."

"Why?"

"It seems weird to me that Heavenly Father would get involved in a little test of wills like that," Ammon said. "You think he would simply want everyone to make it safe, you know? I wouldn't think it would matter to him who got there first."

"I see your point," Sariah said. "But there are two ways to look at it. One, maybe Cornelius needed to be taught a lesson."

"True," Ammon admitted. "I think he did."

"And two," Sariah continued. "I think the Lord was showing Mary—and us, for that matter—that if you have enough faith, He will help you achieve you righteous goals."

"Can't argue with that," Ammon said. "Still, back to the task at hand, how does all of that make Mary Fielding Smith Cornelius's bane? It sounds like it was the other way around."

"Imagine how embarrassed he was to have been beaten to Salt Lake by her."

"True," Ammon agreed.

"Then there's the fact that he has kind of gone down in church history as a villain, because of his interactions with her," Sariah continued.

"Yeah, I guess that too."

"I think Mary Fielding Smith perfectly qualifies as Cornelius's bane," Sariah concluded.

"Hmm let me see, a woman who is stubborn beyond reason and disregards the advice of the males in her life. Sounds familiar," Ammon jibed.

"If you are inferring that I am like her, I would take that as a supreme compliment. Mary always was one of my heroes. Her example of faith and her willingness to endure to the end shaped the destiny of the church for generations."

"How's that?" Ammon asked.

"Her son, and later her grandson, became presidents of the Church. Both cited her as a major influence in their lives."

"Wow!" Ammon said. "That's quite a track record."

"In spite of your doubts, I took the liberty of already writing fourteen and thirteen in their appropriate spots."

$$12\,T\,0\,5\,\_\,6\,5\,1\,0.14\,ME$$
$$4\,5\,1\,7\,1\,\_\,\_.13\,MN$$

"Fantastic!" Ammon respond, when Sariah showed him the paper. "Only two more riddles. That last one was easy. We didn't even have to go anywhere."

"That's because we have the Internet. Imagine trying to find this stuff without it. I don't think we would be past square one."

"True," agreed Ammon. "I guess it's a good thing we are twenty-first century treasure hunters."

Sariah laughed and nodded but Ammon could see worry starting to creep into his wife's eyes. The reason for her anxiety was not difficult to surmise.

"You worried about your dad?"

"Yeah."

"Why don't you call his satellite phone?"

"I tried while we were driving. No answer."

Ammon sighed and tried to reassure Sariah, "I'm sure he's okay. There's nothing he can't handle."

"I know. I just wish I knew where he was."

"Well…" Ammon said trying to sound cheerful and hide his own concern. "Let's finish this little crossword puzzle and go find him!"

Sariah nodded. "All right, what's the next one say?

28

1521 A.D.

Tlahuicle placed his bag on the ground, leaned against a tree, and struggled to catch his breath. Of all of the new lands he had visited on this quest, this was the strangest and most difficult. The mountains reached so high, the trees ceased to grow on them. Snow lay upon the ground even though it was well into summer. The chests of the strongest men burned the higher they climbed. This was the land of legend. It was fitting that his mighty ancestors came from such a place.

The two Nuche guides were not as affected by their surroundings as the Aztec men. It was fortunate that they accompanied them on this last leg of the journey. The trail of the Old Ones was increasingly hard to follow. Tlahuicle doubted whether he would have found his way without them. There were so many rocks, so many lakes, and so many trees. It would be too easy to become lost and never reach his sacred destination.

Despite the hardships, Tlahuicle was moved by the rugged beauty of this place. If only he and his beloved Acaxochitl could have walked the forest together and held each other under the starry skies. If only they could have bathed their children in the clear streams and played games with them in the flower-strewn meadows. It was not to be.

Tlahuicle rubbed his sore shoulder. *Soon*, he told himself as he lifted the bag from the ground. *The Nuche say that we will be there soon. Then I will find my rest.*

29
Present Day

Ammon Rogers watched with a mixture of shock and pride as his wife polished off her second full piece of cheesecake.

"I thought your family just ate ice-cream," Ammon said, wryly.

"That's my dad; I'll take this Lion House cheesecake over ice-cream any day," Sariah responded, enthusiastically. "And oh, you've got to try the rolls here. They are to die for!"

"Don't you think we should be trying to figure out the last two clues?" Ammon asked, gingerly.

"Come on Ammon, I think a busy morning of gun play and car chases entitles a girl to a little break and some cheesecake, don't you?"

"I suppose it does."

"Does it entitle her to some rolls as well?"

"I'm sure that, too," Ammon laughed, "but why don't we work on the riddles first?"

"Oh, all right," Sariah pouted. She removed the sheet of paper containing the riddles from her jacket and read, "Okay…this one here says, *High on a mountain top there are no doubles.*"

"High on a mountain top there are no doubles?" Ammon repeated.

"Yep," Sariah replied.

"What do you make of that? There are a lot of mountains around here."

"The first thing that comes to mind is the church hymn, *High on the Mountain Top*," said Sariah.

"Oh yeah," Ammon said, nodding. "Maybe the answer is in the lyrics somewhere."

"Maybe," Sariah agreed. "Too bad we don't have a hymn book. Should we call Kevin and have him look?"

"No! No need!" Ammon interjected. "I have one in the car. I never took my church bag out of the trunk last Sunday. The car's not too far away, I'll go get it."

"Fine," Sariah said. "That will give me time to buy some rolls."

When Ammon returned to the Lion House dining area fifteen minutes later, he met a scene of utter carnage. A scene of carnage, that is, if you were a roll. Several small plates clustered around Sariah's place, covered in crumbs.

"How many of those things did you eat?" he asked.

"That is a question you should never ask a lady," she replied with mock indignance. "Now, crack open the hymn book. I think it's near the beginning."

"Here it is: page five," Ammon said, sitting down next to his wife. They both silently read the words.

High on the mountain top A banner is unfurled.

Ye nations, now look up; It waves to all the world.

In Deseret's sweet, peaceful land,

On Zion's mount behold it stand!

For God remembers still His promise made of old

That he on Zion's hill Truth's standard would unfold!

Her light should there attract the gaze

Of all the world in latter days.

His house shall there be reared, His glory to display,

And people shall be heard In distant lands to say:

We'll now go up and serve the Lord,

Obey his truth, and learn his word.

For there we shall be taught The law that will go forth,

With truth and wisdom fraught, To govern all the earth.

Forever there his ways we'll tread,

And save ourselves with all our dead. [26]

"What do you think?" Sariah asked when they had finished.

"I don't know," Ammon responded. "I didn't notice any numbers at all."

"Not in the text anyway," Sariah agreed. "The only numbers I see are the tempo at the top and the birth and death years of the two writers, plus the scriptures at the bottom."

"True, but none of those are doubles."

"Hmmm," Sariah said stroking her chin. "Scriptures at the bottom, eh?"

"What are you thinking?"

"Maybe the answer to the riddle isn't in the song. Perhaps this is another riddle within the riddle, like back at the sphinx," She replied.

"And you're thinking the answer is in one of those scriptures at the bottom?"

"Worth a try," Sariah said. "Have you got scriptures in your church bag, too?"

"Of course. I like to look at the maps in the back when the talks get boring."

"Cute. Look up Isaiah chapter two, verses two through three, and Isaiah chapter five verse twenty-six… It's in the Old Testament."

"I know where Isaiah is," Ammon retorted. "Okay… here are the ones in chapter two: *And it shall come to pass in the last days, that the mountain of the Lord's house shall be established in the top of the mountains, and shall be exalted above the hills; and all nations shall flow unto it. And many people shall go and say, Come ye, and let us go up to the mountain of the Lord, to the house of the God of Jacob; and he will teach us of his ways, and we will walk in his paths: for out of Zion shall go forth the law, and the word of the Lord from Jerusalem.*

"No numbers in there," Sariah said.

"Nope," Ammon agreed. "That scripture is talking about the temple right?"

"Yup," Sariah replied. "And notice how the words of *High on the Mountain Top* draw heavy inspiration from those verses.

"Yeah, I saw that."

"Well, what does the next one say?"

Ammon recited, "*And he will lift up an ensign to the nations from far, and will hiss unto them from the end of the earth: and behold, they shall come with speed swiftly:*"

"Ensign…Ensign…I wonder."

"What?" Ammon asked.

"Up behind the Capitol Building, is a place called Ensign Peak. I'm pretty sure there is a monument of some sort up there," Sariah responded. "It commemorates what the pioneers saw as the fulfillment of these prophesies."

"Hmm…and there's a monument on top of that mountain?"

"Yes," Sariah answered. "I mean, it's not the tallest peak around, but you do have to hike up a bit to get there."

"And you're thinking the answer to the riddle could be up there, on the monument?"

"Why not?" She returned. "It fits what we've already seen so far. It's a play on words, a riddle within a riddle. It makes you think of the hymn, but it is really about a place. You could get so caught up in analyzing the lyrics that you don't think about the place. Then again, the hymn and the place are closely related."

"You're right," said Ammon. "It does fit, in a crazy sort of deranged old prospector kind of a way."

"Exactly," Sariah responded, with a broad smile. "Sister Henderson's father has dragged us all over this town today, looking at all sorts of obscure monuments. What's one more?"

"Sounds good to me," Ammon affirmed. "Ensign Peak, here we come!"

30

Donald Kress walked out of the small house in Whiterocks, Utah, wiped his hands on the sides of his blue jeans, and climbed into the pick-up truck parked out front.

"You were right, Arapeen," he said to his waiting companion. "That took me longer than I thought."

"My grandmother is a very stubborn woman," Arapeen responded, shifting uncomfortably in his seat.

Indeed, Donald thought as he started the vehicle. Donald had heard the stories of Utes being tortured to death by the Spanish, rather than divulging the location of Carre-Shinob. He had never really believed those tales, until now. Such extreme measures had not been required with the old woman, but it had been close. Even then, she would only tell him of the main trail the Yah-keerah used when taking supplies to the mine. That would be enough: Arapeen should be able to take them the rest of the way there.

This was more pain and suffering caused by John Byrd. If he had given him a true map instead of a bogus one, this unfortunate business would not have been necessary. It had not taken Donald and Arapeen long to figure out that the map was a fake. The mine symbols were all wrong. Donald knew that, based on where they had captured him, the map would put them in the wrong valley.

My old enemy had one last trick up his sleeve, Donald thought. *Or is it his last trick?*

The fact that he did not actually know the fate of John Byrd troubled Don. From his end of the Skype call, he saw Oquirrh turn and heard a shot, but the video chat ended abruptly. Attempts to reconnect with the assassin were vain.

Donald did not know what to think. If John's young companion had killed or captured Oquirrh after he had finished John, it made sense that he could not get in touch with him. Then again, there had been no word on the news of a murder in Provo. Donald was apprehensive, but there was nothing to do but proceed with his plan.

"What… did you do to her?" the young Ute asked reluctantly.

"Oh, don't worry. She will live. She may never play the piano, but she'll live." Donald replied, squinting at his companion.

"Did you really have—?" Arapeen began.

"Hey, partner," Don hissed, "don't get cold feet now. You're the one who brought me here. You hate the Yah-keerah as much as I do. This is the only way to make them suffer like we suffered."

"But—"

"It's too late for doubts, buddy! What are you going to do? Waltz back into Carre- Shinob? Retake your place as a noble slave?"

"No," Arapeen responded resolutely, looking at the floor.

"Oh, Kanosh will be *so* happy to see you, won't he?"

"No," Arapeen said quietly.

"That's right!" Don shouted. "And he's really not going to be happy when he sees me! 'Cause I'm gonna make him pay… gonna make all of them pay! They stole my life, my love, and my future!"

"Those children we saw playing in the park," Don continued, his voice nothing more than a whisper. "They should have been mine…"

Arapeen looked at his companion. Don was breathing heavily, clutching the steering wheel so tightly his knuckles were white. After a moment, the young man said, "Come on Boss, you know I'm with you."

"That's good," Don replied caustically, shifting the vehicle into drive, "because you've got no place else to go."

"Now, what?" Arapeen asked, as they sped out of his grandmother's sub-division.

"We need to find a horse or a mule. I'm not carrying that thing all the way to Carre-Shinob," Donald said, pointing his thumb back toward a very large duffle bag in the bed of the truck.

31

"Pull over here by the park," Sariah said. "I've heard it can be hard to find a parking spot up by the trail-head."

"Where's the trail-head from here?" Ammon asked parking the car.

"I think it's just up the street," She responded. "Do we have any water? It's going to be hot up there."

"It ain't gonna be *Iraq* hot," Ammon said, climbing out of the vehicle. "But yes, we do have some bottles in the trunk."

Ammon and Sariah retrieved water bottles from the back and started walking up the sidewalk. Suddenly, a frantic scream stopped them dead in their tracks. Looking up, they saw a small child running from the park, toward the road. The child's mother was too far behind to catch up. Without a word, Sariah sprinted forward and intercepted the toddler before she got to the street. Sariah scooped up the girl and walked towards the mother, all the while soothing the startled child with big smiles and kind words. Sariah handed her precious cargo off to the grateful mother and rejoined her husband.

"You're going to be a great mom," Ammon said, sliding his hand into hers.

"We'll see," She replied, a twinge of sadness in her voice.

"You will!" Ammon affirmed. "Trust me."

"Okay," Sariah replied, squeezing his hand.

Twenty minutes later, a breathtaking view of the Salt Lake Valley rewarded Ammon and Sariah for their climb.

Ammon whistled and said, "High on the mountain top, indeed!"

"Wow!" Sariah exclaimed. "You can see the whole valley from here."

A flagstone-covered terrace, partially surrounded by a low railing, occupied the summit of Ensign Peak. At several points on the railing, plaques described various historical and geographical facts. The dominant feature of the memorial, however, was a large obelisk fashioned out of rough-hewn stones. On the south side of the obelisk hung a large brass historical marker.

Ammon and Sariah were not alone. Several small groups were enjoying the view and the attractions as well.

"Now what?" Ammon asked.

"I guess, we look around," Sariah said. "Take a look at these signs and see if there is anything about doubles."

"Or the lack thereof," Ammon corrected. "The riddle says there are no doubles right?"

"Yeah," said Sariah. "Whatever *that* means."

Sariah walked toward the railing and its multiple signs and Ammon began to examine the maker on the obelisk.

After reading the plaque twice, Ammon called to his wife.

"What'd you find?" she asked.

"Listen to this," Ammon said.

No 43 ERECTED JULY 26, 1934 ENSIGN PEAK JULY 26, 1847, TWO DAYS AFTER THE MORMON PIONEERS ENTERED THIS VALLEY BRIGHAM YOUNG AND A PARTY CLIMBED TO THIS POINT AND WITH THE AID OF FIELD GLASSES MADE A CAREFUL SURVEY OF THE MOUNTAINS, CANYONS AND STREAMS. IN THE GROUP WERE HEBER C. KIMBALL, WILFORD WOODRUFF, GEORGE A. SMITH, EZRA T. BENSON, WILLARD RICHARDS, ALBERT CARRINGTON AND WILLIAM CLAYTON.

WILFORD WOODRUFF, FIRST TO ASCEND THE PEAK, SUGGESTED IT AS A FITTING PLACE TO "SET UP AN ENSIGN" (ISAIAH 11:12). IT WAS THEN NAMED ENSIGN PEAK. SUBSEQUENTLY THE STARS AND STRIPES WERE RAISED HERE.

"Ok…so?" Sariah responded.

"Look," Ammon pointed. "There are double dates, sort of: July 26, 1934 and July 26 1847. If we take away the duplicate dates, what are we left with?"

"The years, but that number is too large," Sariah responded. "We only have one blank to fill."

"Yeah, I guess you're right," Ammon conceded.

"This is interesting," Sariah said.

"What?"

"Wilford Woodruff is listed here twice," She responded.

"A double name."

"Yes," Sariah said squinting at the marker. "Including the double, there are nine names listed here."

"Take one away and…" Ammon replied.

"…you have eight," Sariah said. "That would fill our one blank."

"You think that's it?" Ammon asked, scratching the top of his head.

"This fits better than anything I saw over there."

"Okay," Ammon said. "But what if we're wrong on this one? This seems like a bit of a stretch."

Sariah wrote the number eight in the appropriate spot and let out a long breath.

$$12\,T\,0\,5\,8\,6\,5\,1\,0\,.\,1\,4\,ME$$
$$4\,5\,1\,7\,1\,\_\,\_\,.\,1\,3\,MN$$

"There are no guarantees that any of these are right," Sariah said, holding up the paper. "We are just going to have to give it our best shot and take a leap of faith."

"Is this our Mary Fielding Smith moment?" Ammon asked.

"Huh?"

"You know," said Ammon. "If we have enough faith, the Lord will help us achieve our righteous goal?"

Sariah smiled broadly and hugged her husband tightly.

"Yes," she said softly in his ear. "I believe it is."

"Okay" Ammon said gravely. "What's the last riddle?"

32

Don't pick up… don't pick up, Ammon thought as Sariah's cell phone rang for the fifth time. After the tenth ring, she hung up and pocketed her phone.

"Darn it," Ammon said, with poorly disguised pleasure. "He's probably out racing his motorcycle or bungee jumping or something."

"Ha ha, very funny," Sariah responded. "I'm sure Kevin has fallen asleep. The guy has been up for over twenty-four hours."

"Yes… Poor guy," Ammon replied, stifling a laugh.

"Oh, so you think this is funny, do you?" Sariah scolded.

"No, of course not," Ammon returned, sheepishly.

"Well, you shouldn't," Sariah continued. "Since neither of *us* can figure out this last riddle, we're stuck!"

"We could call Professor Millbarge," Ammon forwarded. "Nobody knows Church history better than he does. I wanted to call him in the first place."

"Oh you did, did you?" Sariah replied, skeptically.

"Yeah," Ammon responded, with playful defiance. "As a matter of fact, I did."

"Okay, fine," Sariah gave in with a short laugh. "Calling Millbarge *is* a good idea. Do you have his number?"

"Of course I do," Ammon said, reaching for his phone. "I always call him for help with my Elder's Quorum lessons. He doesn't judge me."

"Ammon, my boy!" Professor Millbarge greeted him warmly. "How are you?"

"Not bad Professor, how are you?"

"Fine, fine, and how is your lovely wife?"

"Ask her yourself," Ammon responded. "We're on speaker phone."

"Hi Professor," Sariah said. "I'm well, thank you."

"Oh, hello my dear. Glad to hear it. How's that scoundrel you call a father?"

"He's fine," she answered, flashing Ammon a worried look.

"Good, good… now Ammon, to what do I owe the pleasure? Got another big lesson coming up?"

Sariah shook her head and mouthed the words, *You were serious?*

Ammon nodded and answered, "No. I don't really have time to explain, but we need help solving a Church history related riddle."

"Are you guys on a scavenger hunt of some sort?" Millbarge asked.

"Something like that," Ammon answered.

"I'll be happy to help. Let's hear it."

"Okay, here it is: *Something besides cream is still missing*," Sariah read.

"Something besides *cream* is still missing," Millbarge repeated.

"That's it," Ammon responded.

"And this is Church history related?"

"Yes," Sariah added.

"Well, as cryptic as that is, it's most likely refereeing to Thomas B. Marsh and his wife," the Professor replied.

"Who?" Ammon asked, looking at his wife. She shrugged her shoulders.

"Thomas B. Marsh," Millbarge repeated. "He was the very first president of the Quorum of the Twelve Apostles."

"Really?" Ammon asked. "What does he have to do with cream?"

"You've never heard of him, huh?" The professor said. "That's surprising. Poor old Thomas is often used as the quintessential example of not being offended by small things."

"Oh! I remember his story now," Sariah said.

"Yes, yes," Millbarge continued. "His story is constantly cited in church talks."

"Well…let's pretend for a moment that I missed those talks," Ammon interjected, self-consciously.

"Of course Ammon, of course," Millbarge quickly added. "As I said, Thomas B. Marsh was the first president of the Quorum of the Twelve Apostles, in this dispensation. He was an important man in the church and a good friend to Joseph Smith, but eventually apostatized and became partially responsible for the infamous Extermination Order signed by Governor Boggs of Missouri."

"Really?" Replied Ammon. "What happened?"

"That's where your missing cream comes in," answered the professor. "You see, Sister Marsh had an agreement with one of her neighbors that they would alternate giving each other the milk from their cows. This would enable each woman to make a larger amount cheese at one time than they could with only one source of milk."

"Makes sense," said Ammon.

"Sure," continued the professor. "The agreement specifically stated that all components of the milk were to be turned over to the other sister. The trouble began when Sister Marsh's trading partner accused her of keeping the fattiest parts of the milk for herself."[27]

"The cream?" inquired Sariah.

"Some versions of the story say it was the cream and others say it was the strippings of the milk," answered Professor Millbarge. "To be honest with you, I'm not even sure what the difference is."

"Anyway…" Ammon prompted.

"Anyway," continued the professor. "Naturally, a dispute arose between the two women. This dispute was first taken to the Home Teachers."

"Wow," Ammon interjected. "Home teachers settled disputes in those days? I can't even get the guys in my quorum to go out on a simple visit!"

"Yes, well," Millbarge chuckled. "I can't comment on that, but this dispute was heard by the Home Teachers."

"What did they say?" Ammon asked.

"They ruled against Sister Marsh," answered the professor.

"Uh oh," said Ammon. "I see where this is going."

"Uh oh is right," Millbarge continued. "When the Home teachers ruled against them, the Marshes took the matter before the bishop. When he ruled against Sister Marsh, they went to the High Council."

"And?" Ammon asked.

"When the council ruled in favor of the neighbor, Thomas took the matter before the Prophet Joseph, himself," Millbarge said.

"Let me guess," Ammon said. "When the prophet ruled against Sister Marsh, Thomas left the church?"

"He left it in a big way," Sariah added. "Thomas B Marsh went before a magistrate and swore an affidavit stating the church was hostile towards Missouri."

"That's correct," replied the professor. "And this affidavit was one of the things that led to the Extermination Order, which caused the suffering and death of many Saints."

"All over some cream, eh?" Ammon responded shaking his head. "What happened to him?"

"Oddly enough, he eventually immigrated to Utah and, in a heart-warming story, became reconciled with the church," Millbarge said. "He's buried in the Ogden City cemetery."

"He is?" asked Sariah.

"Yes," Professor Millbarge answered. "I lead a bus tour of famous Mormon graves from time to time, and his is one that we visit."

Ammon's gaze darted to Sariah. Her eyes were wide open and she pointed to the paper containing the riddles in her hand and nodded.

"Well, okay professor," Ammon said. "I think that answers our question. Thanks a million."

"My pleasure. Let me know if there is anything else I can help you with."

"We will," Ammon said, smiling triumphantly at his wife.

"And good luck with the rest of your scavenger hunt."

"Thanks," Ammon concluded and pocketed his phone.

"Tell me what you're thinking," he said to his wife.

"I think we're going to Ogden."

"Why?"

"The wording for one," Sariah replied. "*Something other than cream is still missing.* The word *still* implies that whatever the riddle is talking about is in existence today."

"Or was, at the time the riddle was written," added Ammon.

"Granted," said Sariah, "but as far as I know, there are no structures or monuments dedicated to Thomas B. Marsh other than his grave."

"Yeah, it sounds like he is held up more as a cautionary tale than a hero."

"Exactly," Sariah continued. "And besides, this wouldn't be the first grave yard we've been led to."

"True that."

"Ammon, this is our last clue, and the day's not getting any younger."

"Leap of faith time?" Ammon asked, walking over to the railing and looking out on the valley.

"Definitely," Sariah answered.

"Alright, Let's g—" Ammon stopped abruptly.

"What is it?" Sariah asked, joining her husband.

"Look!" Ammon responded, pointing down to the trail winding up the side of the mountain. A black cowboy hat made steady progress up the path.

"Oh, man!" Sariah exclaimed. "Are you sure that's our friend? It could be someone else."

"It's him," Ammon replied. "I'd know that hat anywhere. How on earth does he keep finding us?"

"It's got to be dumb luck," answered Sariah. "What do we do now? He'll be up here in ten minutes."

Ammon and Sariah backed away from the edge of the terrace. Ammon thought for a moment and said, "I doubt he could have recognized us from there, not with these other people milling about. Let's go off trail around the west side of the summit. There's enough cover that I think we can make it down unnoticed."

"It's worth a try," Sariah responded. They tore off down the west side of Ensign Peak staying in the cover of the scrub oak trees when possible.

When they reached the street fifteen minutes later, Ammon was mad—in fact, he was very mad. He was not sure if the annoying burrs poking his ankles through his socks made him so angry or the continual harassment from this individual, or a combination of both. Ammon had had enough. Seeing the man's beat up truck parked down the street from theirs only worsened the matter.

Reaching their car, Ammon went to the back and popped open the trunk. He retrieved the pistol he had taken from Oquirrh and stuck it in the front waistband of his pants. After John had refused to take the weapon, Ammon had placed it in the trunk, just in case.

"What are you going to do?" Sariah asked, her voice trembling with fear.

"I've had enough of this guy," Ammon responded. "I'm going to finish this."

33

Speeding north on I-15, Ammon Rogers checked his rear view mirror, searching for the battered pick-up truck that had been such a pain in his neck. He had done this several times since leaving Salt Lake City and he had to remind himself, once again, that the man in the black cowboy hat would not be following him. He had taken care of the problem.

"I still can't believe you did that to him," Sariah said, shaking her head.

"I still can't believe you thought I was going to kill him," Ammon responded.

"Well, when I saw you grab the gun and heard the tone in your voice… What was I supposed to think?"

"I didn't say I was going to kill him," Ammon responded, with an impish smile. "I simply meant I was going to take care of the problem.

Thinking of how he had accomplished it, he had to chuckle.

———

Ammon had indeed grabbed the gun from the trunk, but killing the cowboy was not an option. He had something more devious in mind. Ammon sauntered nonchalantly toward the all too familiar truck. When he reached the side of the vehicle, Ammon looked around to make sure no one was looking. When he was satisfied that his actions would go unnoticed, he wiped the pistol and placed in in the middle of the truck bed.

That task accomplished, Ammon walked away from the pick-up and right toward a group of young mothers with children about to enter the park.

"Excuse me ladies," Ammon said. "I don't want to alarm anyone, but I was walking by that truck over there and I saw a gun in the bed, out in the open…"

Ammon had a whole speech about the gun being a safety hazard with so many children in the area, but he never got the chance. Before he could even finish, every woman in the group produced her cell phone and was dialing 911.

"Should we get out of here?" Sariah asked him, as he climbed into the passenger side of the car.

"No," Ammon responded. "Start up the engine but don't leave. I want to see what happens."

It was not five minutes before the first police officer arrived on scene, followed a short time later by two more. Ten minutes after that, a tow truck appeared.

"Boy, they aren't messing around, are they?" Sariah commented.

"I think the proximity to the Capitol helped get their attention," he responded.

"What do you think our friend will do when he sees his truck missing?" Sariah asked.

"We'll know in a second: here he comes!"

As the cowboy came into view, the sight of the Police around his truck stopped him dead in his tracks. Once the initial shock wore off, he started toward the officers as if to find out what the problem was. When he saw one of the officers remove the gun from the truck bed, however, his body language suddenly changed. The cowboy's eyes darted nervously from one side to the other and he pulled his hat down over his face. He turned around and started walking back up the street.

"All right, let's go," Ammon had said.

Sariah slipped the car into gear and pulled away from the curb.

"Want me to turn around?" Sariah asked. "We're going to drive right past him."

"No. It's okay," Ammon responded. "Let's say hello."

––––––––––––

Ammon tightened his grip on the wheel and laughed again.

"What's so funny?" Sariah asked.

"Oh…I was just thinking about driving past our friend back there."

"Yes, waiving at him was a nice touch," Sariah snickered.

"Wasn't it, though?" Ammon agreed. "And he was nice enough to wave back."

"Yeah, but he looked so sad with his black eye and all," Sariah continued.

"Well, Sione apparently packs a mean punch," responded Ammon.

"All I can say is, I'm glad you're on my side," Sariah chuckled.

"Who else's side would I be on?" Ammon asked, feigning offense.

They laughed together and drove on in silence for a time.

"Still nothing from your dad?" Ammon finally asked. After getting clear of the subdivision, Ammon and Sariah had changed seats. Since then, she had tried to reach her father on his satellite phone several times.

"No. Nothing."

"I'm sure he's okay," Ammon tried to reassure his wife. "We'll be able to go to him soon."

Sariah said nothing, but nodded.

They were so close! Ammon thought. *One more clue, and then…and then.* Ammon tried to push thoughts of gold out of his mind. He knew that the treasure was slated for a much higher purpose than his own personal desires, but he could not stop thinking about it. It seemed so close.

"Sariah?" Ammon asked, his thoughts of Carre-Shinob reminding him of something he had meant to ask.

"Yes."

"I can't remember now if it was you or your dad who said this, but it was brought up that not only did the Aztecs take treasure to Carre-Shinob but also… sacred relics?"

"Yeah," Sariah responded.

"What kind of relics?"

"Scholars and researchers don't know for sure; it has been speculated that the most important thing they hid away were their records."

"Records?" Ammon repeated.

"Yeah," Sariah continued. You know, their records. The ones containing their history dating back hundreds if not thousands of years. Very ancient stuff."

"Would they date back to the time when the Aztecs lived in the north?"

"I'm sure," Sariah replied. "A study of their records would put to rest any speculation concerning their origin and probably shed light on their belief in Quetzalcoatl."

'Why would they have wanted to hide them?"

"Because the Spanish would have destroyed them, if they hadn't."

"Really?"

"Oh yes," Sariah said, gravely. "The priests who accompanied the Conquistadors destroyed everything they felt contradicted their Christian faith. The considered the records of the Mesoamerican people evil because they pictured strange gods and detailed human sacrifice. A priest named Diego de Landa almost single handedly destroyed the Mayan language by burning thousands of hand written books."[28]

"Ouch!"

"Ouch is right," said Sariah. "It's ironic, really; if the friars had bothered to study the text, they would have found Mesoamerican beliefs not as pagan as they thought."

"How so?"

"The Spanish found the oral tradition of the people contained numerous Christian beliefs and practices including baptism, the sacrament, a version of the ten commandments, and circumcision, to name a few."[29]

"And, of course, the belief in a white god coming down from heaven," added Ammon.

"Well, the significance of that wasn't understood until later, now was it? Who knows? If they had not burned the vast majority of the books, it might have been, but that's all conjecture. The fact is, the Spaniards destroyed any Aztec, Mayan, or other records that fell into their hands, and we will never know what they said. Records kept on golden plates were especially at risk, like the ones said to be hidden in Carre-Shinob: anything gold they melted down right away and shipped back to Spain."

"Ancient records on gold plates, eh?" Ammon laughed.

"Yeah, go figure. You know, it always cracks me up me how mainstream scholars say there is no ancient written evidence of the Book of Mormon, while knowing full well the Spanish torched all of the books."

"How convenient."

"Yup. Anyway," Sariah went on, "there is supposedly other stuff in there, too."

"Like what?"

"As well as being a repository for treasure and ancient records, it is said that Carre-Shinob is also a sacred burial site."

"No kidding?"

"Yeah. Most Utah historians know after Chief Walker died, they buried him in a rock tomb in Rock Creek, near Manti. Most historians don't know his body was later moved to Carre-Shinob."

"Really?" Ammon asked.

"Yeah, Isaac Morley…"

"Remind me who he was again."

"He was the guy Walker saw in the vision; you know, the first white man to go there," Sariah said.

"Oh, yeah!"

"Right. In his journal, he described the removal of Walker's remains from the rock tomb and their final interment in Carre-Shinob. He even dedicated the final resting spot using the priesthood."

"No kidding?" Ammon was incredulous.

"There is some corroborating evidence for this story," Sariah added. "In the 1930's, a noted Utah historian found and opened what, he assumed, was Walker's tomb on Meadow Creek."[30]

"Let me guess," Ammon said. "It was empty?"

"Yup," Sariah responded.

"Interesting."

"Very. It is also interesting to note Isaac Morley wrote in his journal that Walker was not alone."

"Oh?"

"Yeah," Sariah continued. "Morley said other, more ancient, chiefs were already there."[31]

"Wow," Ammon said. "Walker is in Carre-Shinob, huh?"

"Yup," Sariah said, glancing at a passing road sign proclaiming seventeen miles to Ogden. "I'll introduce you to him when we get there."

34

"Ammon," Sariah called to her husband. "Come here."

"Find it?" Ammon asked, eagerly joining his wife's side. They had been searching for Thomas B. Marsh's grave for over an hour.

"No," she replied, cheerlessly. "Something else."

Cemeteries, by their very nature, are melancholy places. Sariah, however, had found a place in the Ogden City Cemetery that was more melancholy than usual. Surrounding the young couple were dozens of small grave markers, spaced only a few feet apart. This was a burial place of very small children.

"Look," Ammon said. "They don't even have first names. The markers simply say 'Baby,' the family name, and then a year."

"Maybe they were still born or died shortly after bir—th," Sariah's words caught in her throat.

Ammon turned to Sariah and saw her eyes wet with tears.

"Hey, you okay?" he asked.

"Yeah," replied Sariah. "It's just—I go around feeling sorry for myself because we haven't had any luck. Then I see this and think of a those poor moms, you know, carrying the babies that whole time. Hoping and dreaming for them and then losing them so soon. They didn't even have time to name them. It—it—"

"Puts everything into perspective?" responded Ammon, placing his arm around his wife.

"Yeah," Sariah concurred. "I'm all right. Let's get back to work."

"It's too bad that we don't have a map of this place," Ammon said. "Still no luck getting in touch with Kevin?"

"No. Still no answer," Sariah responded. "Millbarge?"

"Negative. I think he usually goes to the temple today. We should have gotten better instructions from him when we had the chance."

"I guess we keep looking," Sariah responded. "Should we split up again?"

"We could, or maybe we could ask that guy over there," Ammon said, pointing.

"Why would he know?" Sariah asked. "We've seen other cyclists and joggers and you didn't ask them."

"He's wearing a name tag. Maybe he works here."

"Oh, you're right. What have we got to lose?"

"Excuse me, sir," Ammon called out, as he and Sariah walked toward the man.

"Yes?" the man said, turning around. Ammon saw the name 'Wes' written under the name of a mortuary.

"Do you work here, by any chance?" Ammon asked.

"No, I'm afraid not," he responded congenially. "Are you looking for a grave?"

"Yes," Sariah responded. "How did you know?"

"Oh that's a common pursuit, in such a large cemetery. Tell me which grave you're looking for and maybe I can help."

"How?" Asked Sariah.

"I actually spend quite a bit of time here. I work for a local mortuary, as I am sure you see on my nametag here, and I often come here to help prepare for funerals. I also live close by and love to ride bikes here with my family. Furthermore, I am a bit of a history buff. Try me."

"Okay," Ammon responded. "We're looking for Thomas B. Marsh's grave."

"Oh," Wes smiled. "That's an easy one! Brother Marsh is laid to rest only a few streets away, over on Third Avenue. It's a relatively tall gray marker on the east side of the road, about mid-block."

"Wow, thanks!" Ammon responded. "You really do know your way around."

"Don't judge that until you give me a hard one. Thomas B. Marsh is one of the most famous, er, *residents* of the Ogden Cemetery. Did you know he was the first President of the Quorum of the Twelve Apostles and left the church over a dispute over some cream? He eventually came to Utah and…"

As Wes turned and gestured toward the mountains, Ammon quickly leaned over a whispered in Sariah's ear, "Does everyone know this story except for me?"

"Isn't that usually how it is?" Sariah teased.

"… and that is how President Marsh came to be buried here in Ogden," Wes finished.

"Interesting," responded Sariah.

"Indeed," responded Wes cheerfully. "Is there anything else I can help you with?"

"No," Ammon said, shaking Wes's hand. "You've been more help than you can possibly imagine."

"Great. Have a nice day," Wes replied and then turned and walked away.

A moment later, Ammon and Sariah were standing in front what they hoped was the answer to the last riddle.

"All right," Ammon began. "Says here: *Thomas B Marsh, First President of the Council of Twelve Apostles of the Church of Jesus Christ of Latter-Day Saints, Born Acton Mass Nov. 1 1799, Died Ogden Utah Jan. 1866*"

"Look," Sariah pointed. "The actual day of death is missing. It lists the year, but not the day."

"*Something besides cream is still missing*," Ammon repeated the riddle. "You've got to be right, but what is the date?"

"I don't know."

"It's too bad that Wes guy left," Ammon said. "I have a feeling he just might know it."

"Maybe, but what do we do now?"

"I have no idea," Ammon responded. "Maybe we could…"

Sariah's phone began to ring. She grabbed it from her pocket and said, "Hey, it's Kevin."

"Wonderful," Ammon said through clenched teeth. He almost meant it.

"Hey beautiful," Kevin said, sounding groggy. "I saw that you tried to call me. Miss me that much, huh?"

"You're funny," she retorted. "Where have you been?"

"Fell asleep, I guess," Kevin admitted. "Need something else looked up?"

"We actually do," said Sariah. "You're timing is perfect."

Ammon pantomimed sticking his finger down his throat. Ignoring him, Sariah went on, "Can you look up the day Thomas B. Marsh died?"

"Thomas B. Marsh," Kevin repeated. "Let's see: looks like he died January 31, 1868."

"The thirty-first?" Sariah double-checked.

"Yup, the thirty-first. Did you know he was the first President of the Quorum of the Twelve Apostles and apostatized because of some milk?"

Ammon rolled his eyes. Sariah smiled and replied," Yes, we are very familiar with that tale by now."

"Okay, then," Kevin said. "Anything else, gorgeous?"

"Thanks, Kevin, but I think that's all," Sariah returned.

"Yeah, thanks Kevin. I'm most likely going to beat you up the next time I see you," Ammon called out.

Kevin laughed nervously and terminated the call. Sariah pocketed her phone and retrieved the document containing the riddles.

"Thirty-one," she said triumphantly. "That fits perfectly. The last one is a double blanker."

Sariah wrote the last two numbers in their places.

12 T 0 5 8 6 5 1 0 . 1 4 ME

4 5 1 7 1 3 1 . 1 3 MN

Ammon looked at the paper and its now-complete coordinates, and let out a long breath. He reached into his pocket and pulled out his handheld GPS unit.

"Let me change the settings to the UTM system, name our destination, and get these in there," he said.

He carefully entered the hard-won information into the device. After what seemed an eternity to Sariah, Ammon finally spoke.

"Okay, now all I have to do is go to the FIND function and voilà..."

Sariah crowded closer to see the display. Her heart skipped a beat. Clearly visible on the illuminated screen were the words, *108 miles to Carre-Shinob.*

35

"Are you sure this is a good idea?" Sariah asked her husband, as she watched the sun slide below the western horizon, the trail in front them now fully engulfed in shadow.

"Not really, no," Ammon responded, clicking on his headlamp. "Traveling through mountainous terrain in the dark is not my first choice, but…"

"I know," Sariah interrupted. "We don't know how much time we have left."

"That's right. Donald could already be there, for all we know. We've got to get to Carre-Shinob as soon as possible."

"And find my dad."

"Exactly," Ammon replied. "Don't worry, we can do this. I used to conduct night operations in Iraq all the time."

"Wearing night-vision goggles," Sariah pointed out.

"Yes."

"And carrying big guns."

"Yeah, that too."

"Supported by helicopters with missiles on them."

"Yup," Ammon laughed. "But other than those minor differences, this is exactly the same situation."

"Good," Sariah laughed as well. "We have nothing to worry about, then."

Ammon and Sariah had left Ogden immediately after obtaining the last number and completing the coordinates. They made their way directly toward Roosevelt and on to the town of Whiterocks, nestled in the foothills of the south slope of the Uintahs. They stopped only for fuel and supplies needed for the expected night march. From Whiterocks, a series of dirt roads of decreasing quality led them toward Chepeta Lake which, according to Ammon's GPS, was only a few miles west of the lost mine. It was dusk when they arrived.

Ammon scanned the trail ahead with his headlamp and strained his ears for any sound. With every step he took, he felt himself getting closer to the gold. With every step, the battle inside raged more fiercely. *Why shouldn't I be able to take some of the gold? After all, John has old Spanish gold; why can't I? Is Don right? Is John keeping it all for himself?*

Ammon shook his head to clear his thoughts. *What am I thinking? John is not a greedy man. He is one of the most amazing men I have ever met. There has to be a story to all of this.*

"Sariah," Ammon said.

"Yes?"

"What is the story behind your dad and his gold? I would really like to know."

"Are you thinking about what Don said about him keeping it all to himself?"

"I guess," Ammon admitted. "But I know it's not like that. I know Don was trying to sow mistrust. I just want to know."

"Fair enough," Sariah replied. "My dad doesn't like to talk about it much, and you can see why. We're in this mess now because of it, really."

"Yeah," Ammon said, nodding. "I hadn't really thought of it that way."

"Anyway," Sariah continued. "To make a long story short, Dad found an old Spanish mine when we were living among the Havasupai."

"With Kohat?" Ammon asked, remembering fondly the Havasupai chief he had met when the search for the glowing stones had taken them to the Grand Canyon.

"Yes. If you remember, we lived with them while my father studied their folklore. But you know my dad; he also spent a lot of time exploring the nearby canyons. On one such side trip, he discovered a mine that carefully hidden by the Spanish miners. It contained a considerable amount of gold in bar form, along with the remains of hundreds of Indian slaves."

"The remains of slaves?"

"Oh, yes," Sariah said, adamantly. "I told you before; thousands upon thousands of Native Americans were literally worked to death in the mines."

"That's harsh."

"You ain't a-kiddin'," Sariah responded. "The Spanish even had a book called the *De Re Metaliica*, published in 1555, which detailed the best ways to torture slaves in order to get the most work out of them.[32] The appalling practices advocated by the book shortened the work life expectancy of a Native American mine slave to only a few months. Men, women, children—it was all the same. They all suffered and died."

"Why did the natives put up with it?" Ammon asked.

"They didn't always," answered Sariah. "There were many different Indian revolts, over the years. The Indians drove the Spanish out of the Indian lands, with great loss of life on both sides. The Indians hid the mines and the treasure, hoping never to see the greedy white men again, but they always returned. The Spanish always returned."

"Is that what happened with the mine your dad found? Was it hidden by the Indians?"

"Although that was a very common practice," Sariah replied, "the presence of native remains makes me think that the Spanish hide this mine. The Native Americans would have buried their own."

"The Spanish hid mines, too?"

"Yes, if they sensed an uprising, or were lucky enough to live through one, they would hide their treasure, hoping to one day return for it. Sometimes they did. Sometimes they never made it back."

"And your dad found one of these? "What did he do?"

"Well, to the great surprise of Kohat, he went straight to the Havasupai and informed them of his discovery. He wanted them to know he had found some of their ancestors who were in need of a proper burial."

"Kohat was surprised by this?" asked Ammon.

"Oh yes," Sariah responded. "He had never met a white man who cared more about Kohat's people than gold. He was amazed. Why do you think he later trusted *us* with the information he did? We would have never found the lost stones without him."

"I had no idea," Ammon said. "What happened after John told them?"

"They were so grateful to my father that, after they had taken care of their ancestors, they gave my dad much of the gold in the mine. He did not want to accept it, but Kohat was not to be denied. He said he knew my father would put it to good use."

"Wow," Ammon replied. "That certainly is a different version of events than what is floating around in Don's head, isn't it?"

"Ya think?" Sariah snorted.

"Cool," said Ammon. "I didn't even know there was gold in the Grand Canyon."

"Oh, there's gold all over the west," Sariah said. "The United States Forest Service doesn't want you to know about it, though. They even officially deny that there is gold up here in the Uintahs,[33] but we know from historical accounts that it's here. The Thomas Rhoades story alone proves gold is out there."

"Yeah, your dad mentioned that," Ammon agreed. "Hey, speaking of your father, you started telling me back in Salt Lake where your dad is from and we got interrupted— again!"

"You're right," Sariah laughed. "With all the excitement, I never got back around to it."

"Well?"

"Okay," Sariah began. "My father is from…"

Ammon stopped dead in his tracks. Sariah collided roughly into his back. The tingling sensation at the base of his skull, which had so often saved him, had sprung to life. Without knowing why, Ammon handed the GPS to Sariah and pushed her gently into a clump of small trees growing thickly alongside the trail.

"Hey!" Sariah gasped as she vanished.

Ammon suddenly heard footsteps pounding around a bend in the trail. A powerful flashlight instantly blinded him. He heard the sound of a gun cocking, followed by a familiar voice.

"Hey there, partner. Fancy meeting you here," Travis Stanwick said coldly. "That was a pretty nifty trick back there with my truck."

36

1521 A.D.

Tlahuicle waved his farewell to the last of the royal porters as they made
their way carefully down the rocky slope. The first of the men to leave
the scared cave were already barely visible among the rocks and trees below. After depositing their burdens carefully inside, many left straightway,
eager to rejoin their Nuche wives. Others tarried in order to pay their
respects to Tlahuicle. All were honorable men who had fulfilled their obligation to their master. All deserved the rest waiting for them on the shores
of Lake Under-the-Shadow in Timpanocutiz.

He, too, would have his rest, but here in the mountains among the
sacred treasure of his people. Perhaps one day, his master, Montezuma,
would defeat the men from across the sea and call for his return. He could
then make his way back to the Imperial city.

Tlahuicle rubbed the back of his head and surveyed the rugged landscape before him. As pleasant as such thoughts of return were, he reminded himself of their vainness. He doubted very little the end of his
civilization. If it were not so, unencumbered runners, bearing the news of
Montezuma's victory, would have easily caught up with the heavily laden
men. Such messengers never arrived. The light of the Aztec people was
extinguished.

At least, Tlahuicle reminded himself, thinking of the sacred records
now hidden safely in the mountain behind him, *their story will not be forgotten. I have successfully completed my task. I have come to the end of my journey.*

He reached into the neck of his robe and retrieved the disk of gold that
hung around his neck. Although the magnificent quetzal feathers that had
once adorned it were no more than skeletons, the figure of the winged
serpent had not lost its luster, nor had his memories of the woman who
had placed it around his neck.

Tlahuicle smiled, replaced the necklace inside his clothing, and, thinking of his beloved Acaxochitl, strode into the sacred cave and claimed his place among the legends.

37

Present Day

Of all of the injuries Ammon Rogers ever sustained while playing football, getting the wind knocked out of him was his least favorite. It did not have the sudden acute pain of a sprain or the long grinding rehab of a tear, but it did offer you a period of time where you literally thought you were going to die.

That was exactly how Ammon felt right now. Not long after his capture, rough hands had thrown him to the ground near a campfire. His mouth full of dust and his ears full of scornful laughter, Ammon struggled for breath. Disoriented as he was, he realized that this camp was very close to the trail. He guessed they might have walked right into it. That would have been a disaster. At least Sariah and the GPS were safe.

His head clearing, Ammon observed the faces of the small group gathered around the fire: mainly men, with a few women in the company. They varied in age, but all held one thing in common: the same desperate, greedy, mistrustful look Ammon remembered from the eyes of his pursuer earlier that day, a look intensified now as he stood jeering at Ammon.

Ammon corrected himself. Not all of the expressions were forbidding and hungry. A young Native American across the fire from him wore an expression of anguish, not malice. In the dancing light of the fire, Ammon saw another face, creased in concern. . He looked familiar, but the undulating shadows made it hard to see him. The shadowy man began to rise to help Ammon, but someone pushed back into his seat

"John!" Ammon cried, the cobwebs finally clearing from his head. He tried to get up, but someone pushed him into a sitting position on the ground.

"Hello, my boy," John responded, cheerfully.

"So ya know each other do ya?" sneered Orson Campbell.

"I told ya, Orson," Travis Stanwick burst in. "They was all in that house in Provo together. I missed the old man and the Indian, but ended up chasing this one and his little missy all over Salt Lake!"

"And he done got the better of ya, too," a voice from the group scoffed.

"Whatever. I kept a-findin' them. I could tell they was visiting old Mormon places, so I just kept a-checkin' the ones I knew," Travis countered. "It wasn't hard. Would have got 'em too, if that gun hadn't showed up in my truck and the cops came."

Sporadic laughter peppered the group.

"I still owe you for that," Travis said, bitterly. He looked directly at Ammon and patted the butt of the pistol hanging in a holster around his waist.

"And now, he's here and reunited with his friend, John Byrd," Orson added. "No coincidence, I reckon."

"Oh there ain't no doubt about that!" Travis hollered. "He and his lady friend were up to somethin'! Traipsing around town with a map. I saw 'em! Where is she now, huh? Where is your little missy now?"

"I left her home," Ammon responded.

"Why?" Travis asked, skeptically.

"She wouldn't be able to handle the trip," Ammon answered. "These mountains are tough."

Ammon saw John lower his head to conceal a smile. He knew his daughter would take great exception to that particular fib. Ammon hoped that wherever she was, Sariah had not heard it.

John, guessing that Sariah was around somewhere, discreetly pointed to the back of his neck, raising his eyebrows. His son-in-law's warning sensation had saved his daughter before, and he assumed it had saved her again. Ammon nodded slowly.

"Well, what are ya doin' here, then?" Travis continued. "Followin' your map? Lookin' for gold?"

"You already searched me," Ammon responded. "You know I don't have a map."

"Then what are you doin' here?" Orson barked.

"Looking for him," Ammon said, pointing to John. "He's my father-in-law and my wife became concerned when she couldn't get in touch with him."

"You was just with him last night," Travis remarked, skeptically.

"True, but when he ran off with this guy," Ammon countered, pointing at Oquirrh. "We got worried."

"What was ya doin' in Salt Lake, goin' to all those places? Tell me what yer hidin': I'm a desperate man!" Travis asked.

"I'm not hiding anything. John is a historian," Ammon kept his voice calm. "We looked in some of the places he likes to study. They eventually led us here. He loves the Ute people and their folklore, so we figured he might come here."

"That is correct," John added. "As I told you before, I'm traveling with this young Ute in an endeavor to learn the history of his people. We were on the way to visit the site of a Spanish massacre when we, ah… joined your company."

"I know what ya told me. I just don't believe you." Orson growled. "I saw you talkin' to Ol' Mike. We know you're already rich with Indian gold and are comin' to Carre-Shinob to get more!"

"Well, you are certainly wrong there, my friend," John responded. "I would never attempt a trip to Carre-Shinob."

"Why?" asked Travis.

"Why, because of the curse, of course," John responded, matter-of-factly.

At this, a murmur cascaded through the assembly of treasure hunters. John's utterance gave them permission to express forbidden fears.

"Oh, nonsense," Orson replied. "Them's old wives' tales!"

"Not at all," John continued. "Ask young Oquirrh here. He will tell you."

"Uh… yeah," Oquirrh began, reluctantly. "Spirits of great power help my people guard those sacred places. The bones of any white man who goes there will be mixed with the bones of the Spanish who went before."

"Hogwash!" Orson cried. "Ain't nothin' to it!"

The anxious faces of the others revealed they did not share Orson's conviction.

"Then why does misfortune follow those who seek her?" John asked, pressing the issue. "Why are there so many unexplained deaths and accidents?"[34]

Another murmur rippled through the treasure hunters. John's performance amazed Ammon. These people looked like a group of Cub Scouts around a campfire, hearing their first ghost story.

"Don't listen to him!" Orson yelled. "He's just tryin' to scare ya'll. There ain't nothin' to it, I tell you."

"What about Ol' Bill?" a middle-aged man asked. "He had a heart attack right on the trail and the rangers found him later, with his shovel still strapped to his back."

"And what about them fellers whose dynamite just exploded, for no reason?" asked one of the women. "One was killed and one was maimed. For no reason that dynamite went up."

"I heard tell of a fella whose friend was shot and killed by the Indians when they tried to go into a mine hid by a crick,"[35] added still another.

"Then there's my donkey!" another man cried. "Last time I was up here, a tree fell over and killed her."

"Jonathan Calgary," Orson returned, "You are a darn fool! If you hadn't tied her to a dead tree during that windstorm, yer donkey would still be here stinking up our camp! Look at all of you! Ya'll are bein' foolish. There ain't no curse!"

"Be honest with yourselves," John continued. "You can feel them, can't you?"

"Feel what?" Travis cried.

"The eyes of the Keepers of the Yellow Metal and their spirit allies," John replied. "They are watching us this very minute. You can feel them, can you not?"

Not a single soul sitting around the fire answered this last question. Their silence was deafening. John continued to press his advantage.

"And then, there is the Lord," he said in a low voice.

"What about Him?" Orson asked, almost in a whisper.

"Oh, come on folks," said John. "I am acquainted with some of your families. I know most of you went to church when you were young."

"What of it?" Travis responded.

"So," John said. "That means you should know what the scriptures say about hidden treasure. Helaman 13:20 in the Book of Mormon says:

And the day shall come that they shall hide up their treasures, because they have set their hearts upon riches; and because they have set their hearts upon their riches, and will hide up their treasures when they shall flee before their enemies; because they will not hide them up unto me, cursed be they and also their treasure; *and in that day shall they be smitten, saith the Lord.*

John said the last part dramatically. "Think about it carefully, my friends. The curse is real."

Think about it, they all did. A nervous silence descended over the group. Travis was pale as a ghost. Even he seemed to be reconsidering his desire for gold. As Ammon pondered how to make the most of the present situation, the crackling campfire was suddenly extinguished. A large, sodden mass of grass lay smoking in the fire ring, leaving only a small corner of the fire still burning. A shrill, penetrating war whoop issued from the darkness, "Ieh, ieh, ieh, ieh, ieh, ieh!"

The varied effects on the assembled prospectors was instantaneous. Some fell flat on their backs petrified by fear, while others bolted and ran wildly into the woods, tripping and crashing into trees.

Startled, Ammon quickly realized what happened. Seizing his chance, he jumped up from the ground and ran over to Travis, who was rooted to his spot. With one well-aimed punch, Ammon knocked him out cold. Ammon snatched the gun from Travis' belt and fired into the air, screaming at the top of his lungs.

John made the most of the situation. "The spirits! They are coming for us! I see them! I see them!"

John's theatrics sealed the deal. The remaining treasure hunters, with the exception of Travis, fled into the night. The sound of breaking branches continued long after the shooting and screaming had stopped. Well before that, Sariah was in Ammon's arms.

"Not bad for a woman who can't make a soufflé!" Ammon said, fondly.

"Hey, you're not the only one who can pull off a bit of rescuing," She kissed him. "To be fair, my father's prowess as a story teller did most of the work, but I must say shooting the gun into the air was a nice touch."

"Glad I could be of assistance," Ammon responded.

"However, we need to chat later about this whole *me being unable to handle the trip* business," Sariah chided. "And, the next time you shove me into the bushes, a little warning would be nice?"

"They—You—I— Ammon stammered. Sariah winked at him, and then bounded into the arms of her father.

"Daddy," she lovingly scolded. "Why didn't you answer your phone? I was worried sick."

"I am sorry my dear," John replied. "At first, I forgot to turn it on. Then we fell into this lot and they confiscated it."

"You know, Dad," Sariah continued. "The phone only works if you turn it on."

"Yes, yes," John smiled. He turned to Ammon and shook his hand. "Good to see you, my boy. From listening to this Travis fellow, it sounds like you two have had a wee bit of an adventure today."

"That's putting it mildly," Ammon laughed. "We'll have to tell you all about it over a bowl of ice cream."

"Now you are talking, son," John said, clapping his son-in-law on the back. "Consider it a date. After all Oquirrh and I have been through today, I could certainly use some."

"What happened?" Sariah asked.

"Well," John started. "Early this morning, we spoke with an old Ute. I thought he would be able to help us, especially, after we explained the situation to him."

"But he didn't," Ammon guessed.

"No," John said, flatly. "He would not. No amount of entreaty shook him from his resolve."

"What did you do then?" Sariah asked.

"We came up here and wandered around for a long time," John continued with his narrative. "Poor Oquirrh could not recognize anything at all. With a growing sense of desperation we looked, it seemed, behind every tree, but to no avail. Earlier this evening we were… introduced to our friends back there."

"Great guys, aren't they?" Ammon responded.

"Indeed," John chuckled wryly. "We spent a pleasant evening with them, basking in threats of bodily harm unless we told them what we knew. Which, of course, was nothing: our problem in the first place. I did, however, enjoy Travis's rendition of your escapades today."

"Oh, we had such a great time with him today," Ammon added. "We're already planning a reunion with him next summer."

"That said, am I to assume, from your presence here, a successful outcome to your escapades?" John queried. "We certainly need those coordinates. Did you find them?"

"Of course we did, father dear!" Sariah said holding up the GPS, "and according to this, we're only a half mile away."

38

"We are here," Oquirrh's voice cracked with excitement as he pointed to the large boulder twenty feet up the side of the slope.

"We're where?" Ammon asked, scanning the indicated area with his flashlight.

"The entrance to Carre-Shinob," Oquirrh responded.

Ammon turned and looked at Sariah, who gazed intently at the GPS. She looked up and nodded. "This thing says it should be right where he's pointing."

"It makes sense," John added. "People who have been here say the entrance is so well disguised, one simply passes on by."

"Trust me," Oquirrh said, walking up to the boulder. To Ammon's great astonishment, the young Ute vanished.

"I have wanted to see this place for as long as I can remember," John said eagerly, disappearing into the side of the mountain, as well.

"This is sooo cool," Sariah said, following her father.

Ammon stood alone in the dark on the side of the steep hill, his heart pounding in his chest.

"Am I the only one here who remembers there could be enough cesium in there to take the paint off an aircraft carrier?" Ammon shouted into the night. He stepped toward the rock.

Standing next to the rock, and only then, Ammon realized it was not a solid boulder at all. Rather, it was several slabs of rock arranged to form an S-shaped passage into the mountain. A stone on top, expertly shaped and fitted, covered the slabs so the entire arrangement resembled a single mass of rock. The passageway was extremely narrow and the angles very sharp, adding to the illusion. One literally had to be right next to the rock to see there was even a cleft at all.

Snaking through the tight space, Ammon's heart beat faster. He had never suffered from claustrophobia, but the cold stone pressing in on him from front and behind, the wall only an inch from his nose, disconcerted him. Worse, Ammon's mind decided at that moment to conjure up what John had said the day before about death by pitfall.

Coming through on the other side, the others were waiting for him. By the light of the flashlights, Ammon saw concern on Oquirrh's face.

"There should be watchers here," the young Ute said, "guarding the door."

"Even at this time of night?" John asked.

"Yes," Oquirrh responded. "Come, let's go."

As they started to move, Ammon took in his surroundings. Unable to see exactly where he was, Ammon sensed an enormity of space. The group walked up a trail adjacent to a steep drop-off, leaving the stone landing behind. The sound of rushing water emanated from below. Attempting to penetrate the darkness with his flashlight, Ammon barely made out a fast-moving subterranean river a hundred feet below.

Peering ahead in the gloom, Ammon could not see the end of the trail.

He leaned forward and said to Sariah, who was walking in front of him, "I have one word to say to you: Disneyland."

"What about it?" she responded.

"What's wrong with it?" he continued.

"Nothing, as far as I know," Sariah returned. "I've never been there. Why?"

"Instead of going to *yet another* dark, dangerous, cave of death for our next vacation, could we go there? I mean, isn't two in a row enough?"

"I think," Sariah responded, ducking to avoid a swooping bat, "I might get bored in Disneyland,"

"Yeah," said Ammon, "I think you're right."

"Besides, if this way is too scary for you, we could try the back entrance," Sariah continued. "You'd really like that."

"There's a secondary entrance?" Ammon asked.

"Yup," Sariah answered. "That's why there is a nice breeze blowing through here."

"That makes sense," Ammon replied. "Why would I like it so much?"

"Oquirrh says it's high up on the side of a cliff."

"Oh."

"And it can only be reached by rappelling down to it."

"Oooh," Ammon responded. "I think I've had enough rappelling, for a while. This isn't so bad, after all."

"Oquirrh," John asked, "where is the outlet for this river?"

"We do not know," Oquirrh replied. "It flows into a pit below the entrance. As far as we know, there is no outlet."

"Bottomless pit? Great!" Ammon said.

"There are many deep, deep holes here in Carre-Shinob. Some are natural. Some are from mining," Oquirrh responded. "There is even one next to the altar in the temple."

"Temple?" said John.

"Yes," the young Ute said. "The Sun Temple. We must go through there; you will see."

"Fascinating," John enthused. "I can hardly wait."

"You can hardly wait to fall into a bottomless pit?" said Ammon.

"No, my friend." Oquirrh cut in. "There is a bottom. We believe it contains an underground lake. As children, we used to drop rocks down the hole and count until the splash of the water."

"How long did it take?" Sariah asked.

"To the count of fifteen," answered Oquirrh.

"That's reassuring. It might as well be bottomless," Ammon muttered under his breath.

"Why would they put such a pit in the middle of a temple?" Sariah asked.

"It was said in times of old, the rite of sacrifice was practiced by my people. They put the altar next to the hole so the blood of the offerings would run into the heart of the mountain," Oquirrh responded.

"So the pit occurs naturally, then?" John asked.

"It is said so," answered Oquirrh.

They walked on. A few minutes later, John asked, "What is that up ahead?"

"Those are the six gates." Oquirrh played his flashlight over the row of stone doorways, resting the beam of light on third opening from the right. "This one leads to the temple and eventually on to the living area. We need to find Chief Kanosh."

John placed his hand on the young Ute's shoulder and said, "My young friend, how do you think the chief will receive you? Will he be angry that you left?"

"It does not matter how I am received," Oquirrh replied. "If I am to be punished, then so be it. I must warn Kanosh if it is not already too late. Remember, John Byrd, I decided back at the house of your daughter to make amends for my actions. Whatever happens in there, I want to thank you for helping me remember who I am."

"It is my pleasure." John returned solemnly. "It is my pleasure. Now, show us the way, and we will help you make your ancestors proud."

Oquirrh strode purposefully into the third opening from the left. The others followed closely behind. The deeper into the heart of the mountain they went, the keener Ammon's sense of foreboding became. What he saw out of the corner of his eye as they entered this new cavern did not help any.

"Uh guys?" he said, stopping abruptly and panning his light from one side of the cave to another. "There's a bunch of… dead bodies in here."

Ammon had seen his share of corpses during the war, but what lay before him was different. These people were obviously long dead, their skin desiccated and leathery. Ammon felt like every one of them was looking right at him. The ghosts of history and legend haunted these caves. The eerie sensation made his skin crawl.

"And so there are," John breathed excitedly. It was apparent to Ammon his father-in-law did not share his feeling of unease. "Could it be? Is this the fabled burial chamber of chiefs?"

"Yes," Oquirrh responded, reverently. "Our chiefs and other honored dead find their rest here. This is a most sacred place. Please, touch nothing."

"Is this the place you told me about?" Ammon asked Sariah.

"Yup," Sariah responded. "It appears so."

Ammon scanned the cave, amazed at what he saw. Dozens of corpses lined the walls of the cave. Some were lying down, others sitting up, but all were fairly well preserved.

"They all look pretty good for a bunch of…well you know." Ammon said.

"That's due to the cool, dry, air constantly moving through here," John added. "Almost perfect conditions for the preservation of human remains."

"What a minute!" Ammon spotting something unusual among the various Native American artifacts placed alongside the bodies. "That one is holding a book."

"Oh," John looked eagerly. "This must be our very own Chief Walker. That book is a first-edition copy of the Book of Mormon. It was a present from Brigham Young, said to have been one of Walker's favorite possessions. There is even supposed to be a personal letter from the prophet himself stuck between its pages."[36]

"You are right," Oquirrh said softly. "That is Walker. He was a great man."

"I told you I'd introduce you to him," Sariah added, slyly. "Well, here he is."

"Unfortunately, there is no time for pleasantries," said John. "I could spend a week with these fellows myself, but we had better get moving."

There were three large openings at the opposite end of the burial chamber. Oquirrh hurried through the center one. As Ammon entered, he noticed a symbol resembling the sun carved above the door. The tunnel seemed to stretch on for miles. With every step, the tension mounted. A multitude of thoughts rushed through his head.

Are we simply going to warn the Yah-keerah, or are we walking into a radiation plume any second now? Is there really gold in this cave? Other than ornamentation on the mummies, he had seen none. *If there was as much gold in here as they said, would the Yah-Keerah really miss some?*"

John finally spoke, breaking into Ammon's thoughts "Is that a light up ahead?"

"Yes," Oquirrh responded. "We are very close."

The tunnel descended slightly and, as the light increased, their footsteps echoed, resounding in a large chamber of some sort ahead.

So much for the element of surprise, Ammon thought as an orange light flooded the passageway.

"The torches are lit!" Oquirrh quickened his pace. "Chief Kanosh sits on his throne!"

John, Ammon, and Sariah followed his lead. The Ute moved so fast, the others labored to keep up. As Oquirrh stepped across the threshold and into the temple, they stopped dead in their tracks.

"John Byrd and friends, I presume," Donald Kress's harsh voice rang out. "You're just in time. Won't you come in and join us?"

39

Normally, when Ammon Rogers went into a life-or-death situation, he became hyperfocused on the potential dangers, tuning all other distractions out. While a good soldier could not completely tune out his surroundings, the ability to ignore certain smells, sounds, or other non-critical information was a useful skill to have—a skill Ammon usually possessed. As he stepped into the Sun Temple, however, he found it almost impossible to focus on the danger in front of him. He could not take his eyes off the splendor around him, despite the very real possibility of either taking a bullet or exposure to lethal doses of radiation. Of all of the things he had heard about the treasures contained in Carre-Shinob, none of them did it any justice.

The inside of the Sun Temple was roughly as large as the interior of an average sized grocery store. Every surface of the temple glittered golden in the torchlight, including the nine large pillars that occupied the center of the room. Hieroglyphics were etched in the soft metal covered the walls and pillars. Lining the walls, countless stone boxes overflowed with jewelry, coins, precious gems of all sorts, and statuettes made of gold. Stacked in various places were substantial piles of gold bars.

The amount of wealth located at this end of the room alone staggered the imagination. Billions of dollars' worth in gold stood stacked against the walls, like old books at a garage sale. The collective dreams of all of the treasure hunters in the world barely scratched the surface of what was here.

If Cortez had truly known the extent of the wealth that had slipped through his fingers, Ammon thought, *he would have fallen on his sword!*

"Even the floor is shiny," Ammon said, to no one in particular. "This room really was hollowed out of a solid gold mass."

"Yes my friend," Oquirrh responded. "And there are more rooms like this."

Intermingled with all of these treasures, were wooden box after wooden box containing thin golden plates. Upon closer inspection, Ammon saw engraved writing covering the plates. The boxes were roughly three feet square. The plates in them were oval shaped, bearing a hole in the center and resembling a flattened donut. A wooden post protruded from the center of the box, on which the plates were stacked much like a pack of new CDs.[37] Ammon looked over at John and saw that his eyes glued to these stashes of records.

"Look at that one," John said, pointing to a box next to a rather large statue of a man holding a spear. "See what is written there on the top plate!"

Ammon looked where his father-in-law had indicated. The hair on the back of his neck stand on end. Plainly visible, even in the torchlight, was a familiar symbol. It resembled a stylized IHI, its top tilting to the right.

It was clearly the so-called Mystic Symbol. Ammon had first laid his eyes on it in a frozen Michigan cave. The symbol meant simply, *Jehovah*.

"John, that's incredible!" Ammon said.

"It certainly is," John agreed. "It also tends to lend credence to certain theories of mine. It is not only on those plates; I have seen it on the walls, as well."

The group passed the pillars, proceeding further into the temple, and the rest of the room came into view. Two gigantic discs, roughly eight feet tall and a foot thick, faced each other from opposite ends of the room. The discs rested in shallow grooves in the floor, which kept them from rolling. Like the walls, writing and symbols covered these. They appeared solid gold. The sheer weight of these discs, let alone their value, boggled Ammon's mind.

At the center of the back wall sat a great throne made of stone and elevated on a stone pedestal, a large stone altar directly in front. Opposite the throne, Ammon saw the manhole-sized opening described by Oquirrh. The sight of these wrenched Ammon's attention back to the danger at hand, for there on the throne sat Donald Kress. An older Native American man knelt before him, not from any show of respect, but because Don held a gun to the top of his head. Ammon guessed this man was the chief of the Yah-Keerah, Kanosh. Behind the throne stood a young Ute holding a rifle. He wore an expression of mingled shock and scorn. Nearby lay the crumpled bodies of two men, probably the chief's fallen guards.

As horrible as all of this was to behold, the worst sight was perched on top of the altar. Sitting out in the open was the thing Ammon feared all along. Twenty sticks of dynamite duct-taped together, a large digital timer with red numbers attached to one side and wires running everywhere, lay ominously still. Two thin metal bands strapped the case containing the cesium to the bomb. No mistake about it; Ammon stared at a powerful albeit crudely fashioned dirty bomb, which, according to its timer, was going to kill everyone present in under fifteen minutes, rendering Carre-Shinob uninhabitable for generations.

40

"John Byrd, my old friend," Don said, caustically. "You're still alive."

"I am sorry to disappoint you," said John.

"Oh, I'm more surprised than disappointed," Don responded. "After all, if you were dead, you would miss all of the fun we are about to have here. Although, it does certainly look like I sent the wrong Ute for the job. You were right to doubt him, Arapeen."

"He always was weak," Arapeen responded, contemptuously.

"It's all for the better," Don said. "John and I will be together in the end. Which reminds me; you'd better get going. You don't have much time to get out."

"Are you sure you don't need me anymore, boss?" Arapeen replied, already eyeing the back of the temple and the exit.

"I'll be fine. Just shoot anyone who follows you, okay?" Don said.

At that, the young Ute took one last look at Oquirrh, shouldered a sack of gold coins at his feet and headed for the exit.

"Have a nice life," Don called after his partner in crime. "It will certainly be better than ours."

"Donald," John stepped forward. "It does not have to end this way."

"Stay back, old man," Don said, his gun arm tensing. "You don't want to have to watch the chief here die before your very eyes, do you?"

John froze, "Donald, you do not have to throw your life away."

"I have no life to throw away!" Don roared. "You *took* it from me! The Yah-keerah *took* it from me! The church *took* it from me. I'm going to re- turn the favor. In a few minutes, the keepers of the yellow metal and their protector, John Byrd, will die and the Church... the Church... There will be no more Angel Moronis covered with this gold. There will be no temple complex built in Jackson County, Missouri, by these riches. This place will be so desolate not even the bats and mice will dwell here. I will rob the church of its future. I will thwart the very plans of God!"

"Careful!" John shouted. "The scriptures say 'The works, and the designs, and the purposes of God cannot be frustrated, neither can they come to naught.' "[38]

"Quote scriptures all day if you want, John," Donald said, looking at his wristwatch. "But in less than five minutes, the designs of God are going to come to naught, believe me!"

Their exchange gave Ammon time to study Donald's bomb. As the timer went below three minutes, he made up his mind and stepped toward the device.

"Fiddle with it all you want, boy," Don bellowed. "It may not look that sophisticated, but any attempt to disarm it will only make it go off sooner. I'd take what time you have left and kiss that pretty girl of yours goodbye."

As appealing as that suggestion sounded, Ammon ignored the advice and stood directly over the bomb.

"Suit yourself," Don said.

Have to time this right, Ammon thought. Even in the cool air of the cavern, sweat poured down his back.

The timer read one minute.

"Better get that kiss," Donald said.

Ammon looked at Sariah. She looked so beautiful in the torchlight. He hoped this was not the last time on earth he saw her.

Thirty seconds.

Ammon mouthed *I love you* to his wife, and then acted. Reaching down, he grabbed the metal bands holding the case of cesium in place.

"What are you doing?" Donald snarled.

Ignoring the thin metal cutting deep into the flesh of his hands, Ammon pulled each band sideways as hard as he could.

"Stop!" Donald yelled, taking the gun away from the head of the old chief and pointing it at Ammon.

Suddenly the case popped free. Ammon grabbed the cesium with one hand and with the other, swept the bundle of dynamite off the altar and into the pit.

"Nooo!" Donald yelled, looking frantically at the pit and then at Ammon. He raised his pistol to fire, when the world seemed to end. A tremendous and penetrating boom came from below, followed by a huge jet of water blasting out of the pit. The concussion of the blast, combined with the force of the water, knocked everyone to the floor, toppling stacks of loose treasure. The great golden discs dislodged from their grooves and teetered, nearly falling. As the shockwave subsided, everyone struggled to get to their feet.

"Looking for this?" Ammon asked Donald, who struggled to remain standing. "You must have dropped it."

Donald looked. Ammon held the case of Cesium in his still bleeding hand, and stood with one foot on top of Donald's gun.

"Well, Don," Ammon wiped some water off the front of his nose. "It looks like the only designs thwarted today were yours. Do yourself a favor; never bet against the Lord."

With that, a flick of Ammon's foot sent the handgun spinning down into the abyss.

"Oh, it's not over yet, boy!" Donald screamed. "Give me that case!"

Donald stooped, pulled a large knife out of his boot, and lunged at Ammon. Ammon held up the case in front of him as a shield but the impact never came. Oquirrh sprang at Don and grappled with him for control of the knife.

"This is how you repay me?" Donald barked, as they struggled. "I should have left you here to rot with the others! You are too weak for freedom!"

"I will never disgrace my ancestors for you or any other man again!" Oquirrh shouted back.

"Hold this!" Ammon said, handing the radioactive material to Sariah. "I've got to help Oquirrh!"

John had already started toward the two men but suddenly stopped. Coming up next to his father-in-law, Ammon saw why: Donald and Oquirrh struggled dangerously close to one of the unbalanced sun disks.

Before John or Ammon could shout a warning, the combatants slammed into the giant disk. It swayed gently for an instant under the impact. Then, to the horror of the onlookers, it crashed down on Donald and Oquirrh.

John, Ammon, Sariah, and Kanosh gathered slowly around the massive fallen object. For a moment, the only sound was Sariah, quietly sobbing. Almost immediately, other Yah-keerah entered the chamber. Donald had sent them away under the threat of their chief's life, but perceiving the danger past, they returned. Some had even witnessed the demises of Oquirrh and Don. They too gathered around the toppled disk, silent.

"Young one, do not weep," Kanosh finally said. "It is over. You and your family have done a great thing today. You have saved Carre-Shinob. And Oquirrh—Oquirrh has done a greater thing. He has saved his soul."

41

"You'd think if a person saved Carre-Shinob from being blown up, cutting his hands to ribbons in the process, and almost getting stabbed to death for his efforts, he would be able to, you know, pass on having the deepest recesses of his soul purged by a mystical Indian Chief," Ammon said, nervously.

"Relax," Sariah responded, soothingly. "You have nothing to worry about."

Ammon did not share this sentiment at all and was actually quite worried. True, he had come there to protect the sacred mine, and had risked his life to do so, but deep down he never forgot the treasure. He felt it was for a noble cause, but he had never stopped longing to possess it.

When one of the Utes announced that John, Sariah, and Ammon must submit to a spiritual examination by Kanosh, Ammon started to panic. He had not forgotten what Oquirrh had said regarding such examinations. Kanosh had the power to see the deepest desires of a person's heart. Such an examination of Donald Kress had revealed the excessive greed that had doomed him to imprisonment with the Yah-Keerah. Ammon feared what Kanosh would find inside him. He wondered if he would share the same fate as Don.

The display of pomp and ceremony did nothing to assuage his fears. The temple of the sun was now awash in the light of a hundred torches. Chief Kanosh sat sternly on his throne, flanked by a dozen guards holding golden spears, six on each side. Ammon, Sariah, and John stood side by side, in front of the throne waiting anxiously.

"John Byrd," Kanosh said, firmly. "Step forward."

John complied. When he stood directly in front of the throne, Kanosh leaned forward until his face was only a foot away from John's. Ammon watched in wonder as the old chief stared unblinking into John's eyes for one minute, then two. The room was utterly silent.

Then Kanosh leaned back and said so that all could hear. "John Byrd… long have you sought to defend and protect Carre-Shinob. Never has your heart desired riches, but rather has it thirsted for knowledge. Your greatest desire is to study the ancient records contained in this room, and this desire will be granted. Certain conditions I give you, however. You will only be allowed to read for two hours. Furthermore, the things you read must not be shared with the world. The time is not yet come for these things to be made known."

"What about my daughter and her husband?" John asked. "May I tell them of the things I learn?"

"You may," Kanosh answered, "if they are found worthy. They are under the same obligation to tell no one."

"Thank you," John stepped back, grinning from ear to ear.

"Sariah Rogers, daughter of John Byrd," Kanosh said. "Step forward, child."

Chief Kanosh leaned forward and repeated the process.

When finished, he leaned back, smiled and said, "Sariah, daughter of John, never have I looked into the heart of a white person and seen no desire for anything contained inside the walls of this sacred cave. Even your father sought something here. Your treasure is your family, and it always has been. As to your greatest desire, you do not need an old fool like me to tell you what *it* is."

At this, Sariah hung her head in despair.

"Be of good cheer," the old chief said, reaching out and lifting Sariah's chin. "The answer to this prayer may come sooner than you think."

Sariah, not knowing what to say, returned to her place.

"Ammon Rogers, your time has come," Kanosh said.

Ammon gulped, then stepped forward and locked eyes with Kanosh. He felt frozen to the spot. He could not move, blink or even speak. Then the strangest thing happened. Ammon's whole life started playing in front of his eyes like a movie, only in this replay of the events of his life, Chief Kanosh stood by his side, examining every decision Ammon made. Ammon wanted to explain certain episodes of his life, but he could not. The chief was particularly interested in the recovery of the lost stones and the finding of the map in the sewing machine, with its subsequent race to the mountains. When the vision caught up with the present, Ammon could move again. He felt his fear return.

"Ammon Rogers," Kanosh began, "your name and your deeds have hitherto been made known to us."

"Me? How?" Ammon asked.

"Let me say we have a mutual friend. With all of his praise for you, I must admit I was surprised to see that you have longed much for the sacred gold contained in Carre-Shinob."

Ammon's heart sank deep in his chest. *So this is it, huh?* he thought. *I'm stuck here for the rest of my life.*

"But, I also see the reason for this longing. It was the will of Towats that you found the singing rocks. It is also His will that you study them. Ammon Rogers, because you put the kingdom of Towats before your own desires, you may to take what gold only you can carry. Use the treasure wisely. You will receive no more."

Ammon gaped, speechless.

"One final warning I give you," Kanosh continued. "Tell no one else of your gold. As your wife's father will attest, he who owns much gold has more enemies than friends."

Ammon managed to utter his thanks and return to his place next to John and Sariah.

"All of you," Kanosh said to the three of them. "We, the Yah-keerah, thank you for your service. Towats thanks you for your service. Your names will be remembered with honor for generations to come." Kanosh's voice was gentle.

"Your purpose for coming here has been fulfilled. You must never return to this place. Do not try." A note of warning crept into his voice. "You will not remember the way. Please give your maps and electronic devices to me. Attempting to come back will bring you only sorrow." He turned to leave. "John Byrd, you have two hours."

42

"How do your hands feel?" Sariah asked, walking over to her husband. "Huh? Oh, they're okay. These bandages certainly help," Ammon responded. He was having so much fun watching John bounce from one stack of records to another that he had forgotten his wounds. His father-in-law looked as giddy as a child on Christmas morning.

"They patched you up pretty well, didn't they? The Yah-keerah seem skilled in the healing arts," Sariah took a seat next to him against one of the great pillars.

"They'd have to be," Ammon responded. "It's not like they can run off to the nearest doctor's office at the first sign of a sniffle, can they?"

"Good point," Sariah replied. "Anyway I'm glad your hands feel better. That looked like it hurt," She replied.

"A bit, but it was better than the alternative."

"Why pull that case off the bomb? Couldn't you have just pushed the whole thing down into the pit? Wouldn't the underground lake contain the radiation?"

"No, that stuff is too toxic," Ammon answered. "It would poison the water, and this cross breeze would spread anything that came up in the blast throughout the whole complex. It was get the case off, or nothing."

"Well, I'm glad you knew what to do. I was at a complete loss," Sariah said.

"We would never have even made it here without you," Ammon replied.

"Once again, it shows that we do make a pretty good team."

"Always have," Ammon kissed her.

Their attention drifted back to John and his absolute heaven.

"I don't think he has ever had so much fun in his whole life," Ammon said.

"I think you're right," agreed Sariah.

"Sariah, come here!" John shouted. "Look at this! I knew it! I knew it! It is too bad I cannot tell Millbarge about this. I could really settle some old arguments with this stuff!"

"You'd better go," Ammon grinned. "He might pass out."

Ammon watched John excitedly explain his new discovery to his daughter. After a while, Ammon stood and stretched his back. *Sitting on a solid gold floor is not as comfortable as one might imagine,* he thought wryly. As he absentmindedly gazed at a hieroglyphic-covered pillar, another wave of gratitude swept over him. Ammon really could not believe his luck. Less than an hour ago, he wondered if he would ever leave Carre-Shinob. Now, he was the proud owner of nearly fifty pounds of pure gold. Ammon did not know the current price of gold, but he guessed he had close to a million dollars. With that much, he figured he could rent or purchase any piece of analytical equipment he needed. Nothing would stop him from finding out what made the glowing stones tick. He rejoiced in the fact that, if he and Sariah were careful and worked hard, they would never have to worry about money again. If they were ever blessed with a child, Sariah could stay home if she wanted. They could even do some traveling. The future was suddenly full of possibilities he had not dared dream of just a few days ago.

As he was considering which analysis to conduct on the stones first, a sudden commotion arose at the rear of the temple. Ammon walked around the pillar for a closer look, and saw a group of Yah-keerah holding a struggling man. Through the dim light, Ammon saw none other than Arapeen. As they hauled Arapeen past on the way to the throne, Ammon saw he was bruised and battered.

The guards stood Arapeen before Chief Kanosh. He contemplated the young man for a long time. The expression on the old man's face changed slowly from anger to grief and back to anger. At last, Kanosh nodded his head once, and the guards removed the dissident from the temple.

"I'm glad you caught him," Ammon said, walking toward the chief. "I thought he might get away, considering the head start he had."

"No," Kanosh said, sadly. "His flight was slow. He was burdened, as the Spanish of old."

Ammon was puzzled. "I don't follow you sir,"

"When Montezuma was killed by his own enraged people, the Spaniards fled the great city of Tenochtitlan in a panic. The soldiers who left their pillaged gold behind escaped quickly. Those who would not leave their treasure behind were slower and were easily captured and killed.[39] So it was with Arapeen."

"What will you do with him?" asked Ammon.

"He will be punished," the old Ute said curtly. "That is all I will say on the matter. Now, you had better tell your father-in-law he only has a half an hour remaining. I must take my leave of you. Once again, you have my thanks."

Forty-five minutes later, several men escorted Ammon, Sariah, and John down the long tunnel between the temple and the burial chamber. Ammon carried his gold on his back, Sariah held the case of cesium in her hand, and John wore a broad smile on his face.

"I cannot believe what I saw back there!" he said, exultantly. "Some of my theories were confirmed, and some were blown out of the water. My world has turned upside down. I have to get somewhere and write. I cannot wait to tell you all about it!"

"John," Ammon said. "Do you think the secrets contained in those records will ever be revealed to the world?"

"It could be, my boy," John replied. "The scriptures do say that in the last days, many secrets will be revealed."[40]

"What was the coolest thing that you learned back there?" Ammon asked.

"Oh, that would definitely be that Moroni was here in Carre-Shinob!" John answered.

"What?! Moroni was here?" Ammon cried.

"Yes!" John continued, barely able to contain himself. "Do you remember the part in the Book of Mormon where it says Moroni did not think he could write anymore because he ran out of ore? He eventually got more."[41]

"Maaaybeee," Ammon said, cautiously.

Sariah and John laughed, and John continued, "Anyway, this is where he got it. The Spirit led him here and he got all the gold he needed. The event is chronicled in great detail in one of the records I read."

"Carre-Shinob was around back then?" Ammon asked.

"Oh yes," John said. "Don't make the mistake of associating Carre-Shinob exclusively with the Aztecs. It is far more ancient than them or their ancestors."

"How ancient?" asked Ammon.

"What if I told you 'Shinob' of Carre-Shinob is essentially the same as the Hebrew word 'Shin-ob' which means *Most High God*,"[42] John said.

"Wait a minute," Ammon protested. "I thought you said Carre-Shinob is a Ute word."

"I said nothing of the sort," said John. "What I said was, *Where the Great Spirit Dwells,* is their interpretation of the word. *Carre-Shinob*, like many words that crop up in native dialects, is a linguistic mishmash with outside influences: in this case, Hebrew."

"So you're saying Carre-Shinob dates back to the time of the Nephites?" said Ammon.

"Sure," Sariah added. "Second Nephi 5:15 says the Nephites had gold and other precious metals 'in great abundance.' "

"Furthermore, a Nephite influence could explain the original purpose for that altar," John continued. "As adherents to the Law of Moses in the years preceding the coming of the Savior, they would have practiced the rite of animal sacrifice." [43]

"What do you mean by *original purpose*?" Ammon asked.

"Well," John replied. "I think it is safe to assume that the immediate ancestors of the Aztecs used the altar for something other than Mosaic rituals. Ancient peoples feared and loathed the Aztecs themselves for their practice of human sacrifice. In fact, it is said that they would…"

"Daddy, please," Sariah interrupted, "I've had enough for today. Do you think the human sacrifice stories can wait until later?"

"Oh, yes. I am truly sorry my dear," John apologized. "With the records I examined in there, not to mention the linguistic hints, I think it is safe to infer a Nephite connection to Carre-Shinob."

"Amazing," said Ammon.

"Absolutely," said John. "Two years would not be a sufficient time for a complete examination of that place. Two hours was more or less just a tease. Oh, well. I am certainly grateful for the time I was given."

When they reached the burial chamber, Ammon placed his bag containing the gold on the ground to adjust the straps. He saw the remains of a man he had not noticed before. This man was, like many others, seated with his back against the wall. Unlike the others, he was virtually unadorned. They wore gold and jewels and sundry possessions, but this man was clad simply in fur clothing, a single piece of jewelry around his neck. Ammon walked over to the remains for a closer look at the necklace. It was a golden disk, bearing the likeness of a winged snake and trimmed with the ragged remains of feathers.

"That's Quetzalcoatl on that ornament," Sariah said. "And look, I bet it used to have quetzal feathers on it. I imagine it was very beautiful, when it was new."

Without understanding why, Ammon he felt a tremendous kinship with this man.

"I wonder who he was," Ammon said.

"I don't know," Sariah answered.

"I know this room is full of dead bodies and all, but for some reason this one makes me feel sad," Ammon said.

"Why?" Sariah asked.

"I don't know," Ammon continued. "I wonder what brought him. Did he have any family? What was he thinking about when he died? I am sorry; I know it sounds weird. I think I've been underground too long."

"No, it's not weird," Sariah countered. "If he's here, he must have been an important man, even though he is not dressed like it. I'll bet he has a remarkable story."

Fifteen minutes later, the three travelers found themselves on the side of the mountain, watching a beautiful sunrise.

"A truly amazing night," John said. "One I will never forget."

"Parts of it you will," corrected Ammon. "You know, like how to get here."

"I stand corrected," John laughed. "Except for *that*, I will never forget this night."

"We've gotten more out of tonight than just memories," Sariah said, patting the bag containing the gold on Ammon's back. "What piece of fancy equipment are you going to buy first? That glowing rock won't know what hit it!" Sariah paused in thought.

"What?" Ammon said.

"Did anyone else think it was weird Kanosh called them singing stones instead of glowing stones?" Sariah asked.

"Yeah, I noticed that, too," Ammon replied.

"As did I," said John.

"What do you think he meant?" asked Sariah.

"I have no idea," Ammon said.

"Perhaps it is simply a figure of speech?" John posited.

"Could be," Ammon said.

"It struck me as odd." Sariah held up the case of cesium. "Back to more pressing matters: what are we going to do with this?"

"I thought we'd keep it for Halloween," Ammon joked. "It'll make our pumpkins glow for years!"

"Seriously," said Sariah.

"Don't worry, honey," Ammon put an arm around her. "I've got an idea."

"Okay," Sariah said, skeptically. "But it better not get in the way of the little errand I need to run."

43

Mitch Briggs pulled his green and white SUV into his normal parking spot at the United States Forest Service office in Roosevelt Utah and shifted the vehicle into 'park.' His was the first car in the parking lot. At this early hour, making it this far was an accomplishment. He leaned back in his seat and rubbed his eyes with the palms of his hands.

I need some caffeine, he told himself. Weeks like the past one made him love and hate his job as a ranger at the same time. Working outside in the postcard regions of the country had been his dream job ever since he was a bored kid staring out the windows of an over-crowded public school in New Jersey, but the warm months brought hordes of tourists to the mountains. That meant long days for him and the other rangers. He had participated in two search-and-rescue operations this week alone, not to mention myriad vehicle break-ins at trailheads and seemingly endless animal problems. *When will people learn if you leave food out on a picnic table overnight, wild animals get into it?* Mitch moaned to himself. He was utterly exhausted.

Mitch ceased rubbing his eyes, sighed, and tried to muster enough vigor to leave his vehicle and tackle the mountain of paperwork waiting for him on his desk. *I hate coming in so early*, Mitch thought. *I should be out checking the trailheads, but if I don't get those reports done, I'll hear about it!*

Mitch popped open the door and slowly swung his legs out of the SUV. Once outside the vehicle, he stretched luxuriously and sluggishly made his way toward the front door of the station. He stopped before he reached the door. A metal briefcase, the type of protective case people use to transport cameras or other electronic equipment, sat on the front step of his office, a folded piece of paper taped to its side.

"What the heck?" Mitch wondered aloud.

He walked over to the case, a little more energy in his step, bent down, and grabbed the paper off the case. It was a handwritten note, probably explaining how a person found this camera along some trail and did not know what to do with it. He certainly did not expect the actual contents of the note.

"To whom it may concern: This case and its contents are most likely stolen medical supplies. I don't know for sure, because I didn't steal them. The name of the hospital it belongs to is stamped inside the case, but be careful when you open it, because the inner canisters contain Cesium–137. Don't worry; it's perfectly safe as long as you don't do anything stupid. Please see this case returned to its proper owner. Sorry for any inconvenience. Thank you and have a nice day."

Mitch gulped and quickly read the note again. He looked from the note in his hand, down to the case, and back up at the note clenched in his now trebling hand.

Cesium–137, huh? He thought, trying to stay calm and remember his hazmat training. *Forget my paperwork; I have some calls to make.*

44

One Day Later

Willard Loveland meandered leisurely down the sidewalk next to Main Street in Roosevelt, Utah. He had decided several years ago, on his 70th birthday, that there was not much left in life worth being in a hurry for. It was fairly early in the morning, and traffic was light. He saw his destination ahead: two men, comparable in age, seated comfortably on a bench in front of the local pharmacy. When Willard came within hailing distance, the men turned toward him and waved cordially. They seemed to expect him, for though they sprawled on the bench, they left enough room for one more. Willard maneuvered carefully into position and plopped down into his spot with finality; he had no intention of getting up any time soon.

"Ephraim. Bob." Willard said with the easy familiarity that comes through years of camaraderie.

"Mornin', Willard" responded Ephraim. "Missed ya yesterday."

"Yup," affirmed Bob.

"Sorry, boys," apologized Willard. "My granddaughter had her baby the other day. Went to see the little nipper."

"Was this your granddaughter over in Vernal or the one down in Price?" Ephraim asked.

"The one in Vernal—Maddie."

"Oh," Ephraim said, nodding. "She's a real sweet gal."

"Yup," affirmed Bob.

"She sure is," agreed Willard. "And you should see the baby. He's a darling little thing. Cute as a button."

"Is that so?" replied Ephraim. "Guess that just proves what my pa used to say."

"Oh yeah, what's that?" asked Willard.

"The uglier the bull, the cuter the calf. If I remember Maddie's husband, I'd say that was spot on. Awkward looking feller…"

The three old friends chuckled briefly, and then sank into a contented silence, watching people walk past the drugstore.

After a time—whether five minutes or twenty, none of the involved parties cared—Ephraim broke the silence. "Well, you missed all the excitement yesterday, anyway."

"Yup," affirmed Bob.

"Ya talking about all the hubbub at the ranger station?" Willard asked.

"Nope," returned Ephraim. "Don't know nothin' about that."

"You mean to tell me you didn't see all the army trucks driving through town, or hear all the news helicopters flying over the ranger station? They were there most of the day. My neighbor told me all about it when we got in last night." Willard said, incredulously.

"Nope. Can't say I did. Besides, that ain't none of my business." Ephraim, shrugged.

"What excitement are you talking about, then?"

"The mess of strangers wanderin' around town yesterday. They was actin' all funny like, right here at our drugstore; first thing in the morning too," said Ephraim.

"Yup," affirmed Bob.

"What kind of strangers?" asked Willard, looking from one friend to the other.

"Well, first of all, there was this cowboy," replied Ephraim.

"What is so strange about a cowboy, Eph? This town has cowboys thicker than fleas on a dog's back!" scoffed Willard.

"Not like this one," continued Ephraim. "This one wasn't a real cowboy. He was too soft and scrawny for a real cowboy, clothes was ill fitting. You couldn't wear them for real work. No, this fella looked like a loafer *pretendin'* he was a cowboy. Boy, he was real sad, like as he didn't have a friend in the world."

"Why was he so down?" Willard asked.

"Don't rightly know," said Ephraim, with a shrug, "but maybe on accounts of him bein' all beat up and whatnot."

"Beat up?" cried Willard.

"Yes, siree, beaten like a rented mule. He had two black eyes, his fancy hat all bent up and dusty. In fact, he looked like he'd been wanderin' 'round the hills all night, poor feller."

"What'd he do?" asked Willard.

"He walked into the drugstore, not long after they opened up mumblin' to himself somethin' about Indians and gold."

"Indians? Gold?"

"Yes, siree, came out of the store a few minutes later with some aspirin, gulped down half the bottle, then wandered away, shoutin' out to no one in particular that he 'should have been a dentist' " Ephraim shook his head in disbelief.

"Well I'll be danged," replied Willard. "That is strange."

"Sure enough, and then there was the girl."

"Girl? What girl?"

"A pretty little fair haired gal came to the drugstore about fifteen minutes after the sad cowboy went on his way. There was a young feller and an older gent with her," explained Ephraim.

"I don't see what's so strange about that."

"Well, them folks were dirty and tired looking, too, like they'd spent a sleepless night in the woods. They weren't in such a bad way as the cowboy, although the young feller did have a heavy lookin' knapsack on his back. He kept on a shiftin' it about. We wondered why he didn't just take it off. Anywho, the two fellers stood out on the sidewalk, talkin' real low like, while the little missy went into the drugstore."

"What were they talking about?" asked Willard.

"Well, they was whisperin' and all, but Ol' Bob here thought he heard them say somethin' about gettin' out of town as soon as possible with their gold!"

"If Bob says he heard that, I believe him," Willard said. "He can't see worth a darn but his ears are still as sharp as a foxes."

"Sure as shootin' " Ephraim agreed.

"Gold? Do you think the three of them was in cahoots with the cowboy somehows?" asked Willard.

"We was wonderin' the same thing," Ephraim jerked his thumb toward Old Bob.

"Yup," affirmed Bob.

"Dadgum…" replied Willard, forlornly. "Now I'm wishin' I had waited until Sunday to go and see the new great-grand baby. What happened next?"

"Eventually the pretty lady came out of the drugstore, and smiled real sweetly at us. She walked toward her fellers, trying to put a sad face on, but couldn't keep the ruse up very long. When she got to them, she smiled and yelled out, 'Yes!' and burst into tears! She started huggin' the young feller so hard I though his eyes were going to pop out. The older gent commenced to cryin' and clappin' the younger feller on the back. We heard the little gal tell the young feller she hoped the baby had his eyes. She could barely speak 'cause of all her bawlin'."

"You don't say," Willard said.

"After standin' there and carryin' on a bit, they all walked away as cheerful as can be. Later, when the druggist left for lunch, Ol' Bob here asked him about the little gal. He said she bought a pregnancy test, went right into the ladies' room, and came out a few minutes later with a huge smile on her face. He figured she used the test right there in the drugstore's ladies room!"

"She used it right there in the store?" exclaimed Willard. "Ain't never heard of such a thing!"

The three old friends shook their heads disapprovingly. They sat quietly for a few minutes, watching the people and cars going up and down Main Street.

Ephraim broke the stillness. "Guess that little lady really wanted a baby, didn't she?" he mused.

"Yup," affirmed Bob.

The End

Endnotes

1. Kerry Ross Boren and Lisa Lee Boren, *The Gold of Carre-Shinob* (Springville: Cedar Fort, 1998), 77.

2. Boren and Boren, *The Gold of Carre-Shinob*, 1.

3. George A. Thompson, *Lost Treasures on the Old Spanish Trail* (Salt Lake City: Western Epics, 1986), 7.

4. Susan Wise Bauer, *The Story of the World: Volume 2* (Charles City, VA: Peace Hill Press), 314.

5. Boren and Boren, *The Gold of Carre-Shinob*, 3.

6. Thompson, *Lost Treasures on the Old Spanish Trail*, 69.

7. Boren and Boren, *The Gold of Carre-Shinob*, 22.

8. *Golden Rhoades: Search for Lost Utah Treasure,* Written and Directed by Gibran Begum (StoneyBrooke Films, 2003).

9. *Golden Rhoades.*

10. Mark E. Petersen, *The Great Prologue* (Salt Lake City: Deseret Book, 1975), 110.

11. Gerald N. Lund, *The Coming of the Lord* (Salt Lake City: Bookcraft, 1971), 153 and 157.

12. The Gourmet Chocolate of the Month Club. "Chocolate History Timeline." www.chocolatemonthclub.com/chocolatehistory.htm (accessed on August 27, 2015).

13. Boren and Boren, *The Gold of Carre-Shinob, 20.*

14. Clifford Duncan, "Creation and Migration Stories of the Utes" in *Utah's Native Americans,* ed. Forrest C. Cuch, (Logan: Utah State University Press, 2000), 167-224, http://historytogo.utah.gov/people/ethnic_cultures/ (accessed on August 27, 2015).

15. Boren and Boren, *The Gold of Carre-Shinob*, 175.

16. Boren and Boren, *The Gold of Carre-Shinob*, 145.

17. Tim MacSweeney, "Treasure Hunter's University," Waking up on Turtle Island, http://wakinguponturtleisland.blogspot.com/2011/06/treasure-hunters-university.html (accessed on August 27, 2015).

18. *Golden Rhoades.*

19. Friends of Gilgal Garden, Gilgal Sculpture Garden, www.gilgalgarden.org (accessed on August 27, 2015).

20. Petersen, *The Great Prologue*, 109.

21. Lisa Thompson, *Gilgal Garden: An Historic Sculpture Garden Created By Thomas B. Child, Jr. (1888-1963)*, (Salt Lake City: Friends of Gilgal Gardens), 8.

22. Boren and Boren, *The Gold of Carre-Shinob*, 3.

23. John W. Welch, ed., *Reexploring The Book of Mormon*, (Salt Lake City: Deseret Book; Provo: FARMS; 1992), 93.

24. Rick Satterfield. "Salt Lake Temple." Temples of the Church of Jesus Christ of Latter-Day Saints. www.ldschurchtemples.com/saltlake/ (accessed on August 27, 2015).

25. Francis M. Gibbons and Daniel B. Gibbons, *A Gathering of Eagles: Conversions From the Four Quarters of the* Earth, (San Jose: Writers Club Press; 2002) 146–47.

26. "High on the Mountain Top," *Hymns,* no. 5

27. Gordon B. Hinckley, "Small Acts Lead to Great Consequences," *Ensign* (May 1984): 81–83.

28. *Cracking the Maya Code*, first broadcast April 8, 2008 by PBS, Written and Directed by David Lebrun.

29. Richard Graeber, "Christians in America Before Columbus," *Ancient American* 6, no. 40 (2001): 7–8.

30. Boren and Boren, *The Gold of Carre-Shinob*, 47.

31. Boren and Boren, *The Gold of Carre-Shinob*, 47.

32. Thompson, *Lost Treasures on the Old Spanish Trail*, 19.

33. *Golden Rhoades.*

34. *Golden Rhoades.*

35. Thompson, *Lost Treasures on the Old Spanish Trail*, 52–53.

36. Boren and Boren, *The Gold of Carre-Shinob*, 177.

37. Boren and Boren, *The Gold of Carre-Shinob*, 178.

38. Doctrine and Covenants 3:1.

39. Boren and Boren, *The Gold of Carre-Shinob*, 3.

40. 2 Nephi 30:17–18.

41. Mormon 8:5.

42. Boren and Boren, *The Gold of Carre-Shinob*, 179.

43. Alma 34:13.